W E Hamilton

The Time-Saver

A book which names and locates 5,000 things 5,000 at the World's fair

that visitors should not fail to see

W E Hamilton

The Time-Saver
A book which names and locates 5,000 things 5,000 at the World's fair that visitors should not fail to see

ISBN/EAN: 9783337314439

Printed in Europe, USA, Canada, Australia, Japan

Cover: Foto ©Andreas Hilbeck / pixelio.de

More available books at **www.hansebooks.com**

The Time-Saver.

A BOOK WHICH

Names and Locates

5,000 THINGS 5,000

AT THE

WORLD'S FAIR

THAT VISITORS SHOULD NOT FAIL TO SEE.

———

Compiled and Published by

W. E. HAMILTON,

Room 12, No. 283 South Clark Street,

CHICAGO, ILL.

PREFACE AND KEY.

This little book is published because World's Fair visitors need it.

Is is not an imitation. Nothing like it has ever been published. At none of the great expositions of the past was anything of the kind offered to visitors, although there was a demand for it. Since the opening of the greatest of all expositions, thousands have asked for something better than the so-called "Guides," which give only general information.

The Compiler has endeavored to supply this demand. THE TIME-SAVER *names and locates* 5,000 of the most interesting exhibits on the grounds, *grading* them according to their relative importance.

With the assistance of a corps of bright newspaper men a thorough examination of every building and every group of exhibits was made; and about 5,000 of the most interesting things in the Exposition were *located, classified and graded.* In each department the most important, curious and rare articles were selected—the things that visitors should not miss seeing. In each building a common-sense plan of location was followed, in order that the visitor might readily find the exhibits mentioned.

Everything was *inspected*; catalogues, so full of errors, were not used. The system of grading adopted will be explained by the following

KEY.
1. **Interesting.**
2. **Very interesting.**
3. **Remarkably interesting.**

The figures will be found at the left of every exhibit or group graded. This rule has been applied to every department; that is, three classes of exhibits have been selected from each department. The rarity, merit, value or historical interest of the exhibit governs the grade. In a majority of the references a grade is applied to one article. In others the group system is used. The reason for this will be apparent to one who uses the book.

By using the map and index herein, all buildings can be easily located.

There are many interesting things at the Fair which are not mentioned in THE TIME-SAVER. The publisher does not claim that every article entitled to grade is named in this collection. He does claim, however, that *everything enumerated in* THE TIME-SAVER *is worth se ing;* that it is the only book that will save time and money to the patrons of the Fair; and that the man who uses it will know more about the Fair in three days than the "other fellow" can glean in two weeks. Let any man who has spent two weeks on the grounds consult THE TIME-SAVER, and he will find that he has missed seeing hundreds—perhaps thousands—of things of the first importance; and that he has wasted time in hunting for exhibits and then failed to find them. On this test the Publisher risks the reputation of The Time-Saver.

Even to those who do not visit the Fair The Time-Saver is worth many times its cost. It contains much valuable information that cannot be found in any other publication.

In a few instances, exhibits were not placed when the copy went to the printer. Reference is made to this in the proper place.

No exhibitor has paid a cent for advertising in this book.

The Time-Saver is copyrighted, and all infringements will be prevented by the courts.

The Time-Saver is not sold on the World's Fair grounds, the publisher of a catalogue having the exclusive right to sell within the gates all literature pertaining to the Fair. Nothing, however, sold on the grounds will take the place of The Time-Saver, which is the only guide published that *names, grades and locates* 5,000 of the most important and interesting exhibits.

The Time-Saver is sold by all news dealers; at all the approaches to the World's Fair ground, and on all the principal avenues of travel. A copy will be mailed to any address by the Publisher on receipt of 25 cents. Liberal discount to the trade.

Chicago, Ill., May 24, 1893.

W. E. Hamilton, Compiler and Publisher.

TRANSPORTATION BUILDING.

Dimensions, 256x960 feet; Annex, 425x900 feet. Cost, $370,000.

MAIN BUILDING.

In the main building, first floor, the numbers of sections will be found on two rows of columns running north and south through the center of the building. The following notable exhibits will be found, beginning at the north end:

1. Sections 1 to 5. Carriages, wagons, buggies, hearses and other vehicles.
2. Sections 6 and 7. Mexican exhibit. Aztec antiquities. Native costumes and wagons. Rare old painting of the Virgin of Gaudalupe, the patron saint of Mexico.
1. Sec. 7. Native Brazilian canoe, 50 feet long. Models of Spanish forts, peasant homes and arena for bull fights.
1. Sec. 12. Models of vessels showing development of ship building.
3. Model of the great British war ship, "Victoria."
1. Armor plate showing holes made by projectiles.
1. Sec. 13. Elevators to roof; 10 cents to go up.
3. Model of the " Santa Maria."
3. Boat in which Grace Darling went to the rescue of the crew of the steamer, " Forfarshire," in 1838.
1. Model of the Campania, the ocean steamer holding the fastest record between New York and Queenstown. 7

1. Sec. 14.   Model of Memphis bridge.
2. Sec. 15.   Cook & Son's exhibit—Model of Temple of Edfou on bank of the Nile.
2. Sec. 15.   Model of city of Pullman.
1. Sec. 16.   Electric and steam elevators in operation.
1. Sec. 17.   Arbel exhibit of locomotive and artillery wheels in pyramidal form.
3. Secs. 19 and 20.   Bethlehem Iron company exhibit—Full size model of steam hammer, 90 feet high, breadth 38 feet, weight 2386 tons, strikes 125 tons.   Nickel steel ingot, compressed in fluid state, weighing 55$\frac{3}{4}$ tons. Barbette plate of U. S. battle ship, "Indiana," 17 inches thick.   First experimental plate that withstood projectiles propelled at the rate of 2,100 feet per second at Government test in 1891, breaking the shells.   Model of 110 ton steel ingot. Specimen of hollow forging, 67 feet long.   Shafts for steamers   Twelve inch gun 36 feet long, weight 45 tons, throws 600 pound projectile 8 miles.
3. Scene in the Tyrol, with figure of Christ
2. Sec. 22.   Fac-simile of modern American steamer, 4 stories high.
1. Sec. 25.   Models of North German Lloyd steamers.
1. Sec. 26.   Prussian railway signalling apparatus.
1. Model of Hamburg American packet ship.

ANNEX.

The annex is devoted mainly to railway exhibits. As one exhibit frequently spreads over several sections, and as the sub-divisions are too small to keep in mind, the observer will get along easier to begin at one side and go through the entire exhibit, in which the following items of special interest will be found:
1. German locomotives and coaches.
2. Mammoth Brooks locomotive.
1. Pioneer C. & N. W. locomotive.

2. Locomotive weighing 107 tons—largest in the building.
1. Compound tandem locomotive.
2. Locomotive " Midget."
1. Latest street cars.
2. Locomotive " Mississippi," built in England in 1834.
1. Old-fashioned coach and locomotive.
1. Northern Pacific exhibit.
1. Baldwin compound engine, "Columbus."
1. Coach of 1836.
3. Model of steam carriage built by Sir Isaac Newton in 1680.
3. Baltimore & Ohio Ry. exhibit of old-style locomotives.
1. Locomotive "Lord of the Isles," of Great Western Ry., England.
1. Latest English locomotive, sleeping coach and composite railway carriage.
2. Model of Stephenson's " Rocket" and tender, of the old Liverpool & Manchester railway, 1829.
2. Reproduction of " Novelty," a locomotive that took part in the great contest on Liverpool & Manchester railway in 1829.
3. Model of steam carriage invented and built by Joseph Quinot, of France, in 1759.
3. Model of Trevithick's locomotive, 1803.
1. Model of London & Northwestern railway yards at Liverpool.
1. Reproduction of passenger coach of 1836.
1. Elevator snow plow.
1. Railway velocipedes.
1. Track inspection car and track indicator.
1. Rotary snow plows.
1. Original strap rails on which Trevithick locomotive ran in 1804.
1. Ammonia street car engine.
1. First cable-grip car built, and section of cableway.

GALLERY.

In the gallery the visitor should start at the north-

east corner and go south until he reaches the south
end of the building; then cross to the southwest
corner and go north until north end is reached; then
go east to starting point. The following notable
things will be found in above order of procedure:

EAST SIDE.

2. Bicycles of all kinds, including reproductions
   of first bicycles ever used.
3. Boat and steam fixtures built and navigated in
   1804 by Col. John Stevens.
2. African canoes, boats and vehicles.
1. Model of Newport News ship yards and docks.
3. Model of Nicaragua canal, with water in the
   channel.
1. Model of Union Iron works plant, SanFrancisco.
1. Models of European canals.
1 Model of Nord-Ostsee canal.

WEST SIDE.

1. Model of brick manufacturing plant at Weimar,
   Germany.
1. Model of brewery at Gotha.
2. French mail steamer lines exhibit. Six large
   paintings representing arrival and departure
   of steamers, views of ports, exterior and interior of steamers.
1. Old bateau used in French Canadian fur trade.
1. Model of port of Dunkerque and picture of city.
2. Model of the celebrated Forth bridge.
1. Harness and saddlery exhibits.

———

PENNSYLVANIA R. R. CO.

The Pennsylvania Railroad company has a transportation exhibit of its own, southwest of the Transportation building and near the " L " road entrance
to the grounds. In a large building will be found
relics from different parts of the road bed, models

of old equipment of the road, etc. On track near building are:

3. The "John Bull," the oldest locomotive in America, first used on Camden & Amboy railroad in 1831.
2. Passenger cars used on Camden & Amboy road in 1836.
2. The two cars on which the great Krupp gun was shipped from Sparrows' Point. Maryland, to Jackson Park. Weight of gun, 270,900 lbs.; bridge, 47,000 lbs.; each car, 64,000 lbs.; total, 445,000 lbs.

MINES AND MINING BUILDING.

Dimensions. 350x700 feet.   Cost $265,000.

The visitor should begin at the northwest corner of the building and keep west of center aisle until he reaches the south end of the building; then come back on east side of center aisle until north end of building is reached. In gallery, begin at northwest corner and go south, making the circuit. The following exhibits will be found in that order:

WEST SIDE.

1. Arch of cement from Heidelberg.
2. Mosaics in Karlsbad stone. Pocket books and card cases inlaid. Philip Fischer exhibit.
2. View of Carlsbad.
1. French asphalt specimens.
1. French work in gold, platinum and aluminum.

NEW SOUTH WALES.

3. Silver statue of Atlas.
2. Remarkable display of ores, metals and coal.

ONTARIO.

1. Marble and granite.
1. Nickel and copper ores.
1. Graphite and soapstone.
2. Ingot of nickel, weight, 4,500 lbs.; value, $2,250.
1. Platiniferous sand from which platinum is made
2. Piece of nickel ore weighing over 6 tons.
1. Platinum ore.

BRITISH COLUMBIA.

1. Pyramid representing amount of gold taken from mines of British Columbia.
1. Ores of various kinds.

---

1. Canadian asbestos.
1. Canadian ores, minerals and coal.
2. Lump of cannel coal from New Abram mines, Lancashire, England; weight 11 tons, 1,400 lbs.
2. Japanese exhibit (not complete at this date, but will be very interesting.)
2. Statue, "Liberty Enlightening the World," carved in salt.
1. Farnley Iron company exhibit of glazed brick and ware.
3. Pillar of anthracite coal 60 feet high from Schuylkill county, Pa., representing thickness of vein from top to bottom. (In center of aisle.)
3. Stumm exhibit—pillars, statuary, beams and sections.
2. Hand-made water pipe 60 feet long, 3½ feet in diameter. (Fitzner exhibit.)
1. Humboldt ore concentrator.
2. Zinc display of Wilhelm Grills. Statuary in zinc.
2. Russia. (Not complete at this date.)
2. Brazil. (Not complete at this date.)
2. Cape of Good Hope. (Not complete at this date.)

2. Spain. (Not complete at this date.)
2. Mexico. (Not complete at this date.
1. Chili. Model of nitrate of soda works and specimens of nitrate of soda.

EAST SIDE.

COLORADO.

1. Valuable piece gold quartz.
1. County and mining camp exhibits of ores and minerals.
2. Coal exhibit of U. S. Coal company of Denver.
2. Alabaster statue of buffalo.

IOWA.

2. Coal mine and miners at work.
1. Specimens from cave in Dubuque county.
1. Ancient pottery.

NEW MEXICO.

2. Model of miner's cabin.
1. Iron, zinc, lead and copper.

MONTANA.

3. Silver statue of Justice (modeled after Ada Rehan,) height, 6 feet above pedestal; weight, 2½ tons.
1. Model showing system of timbering mines.
1. Minerals and ores.

ARIZONA.

2. Slabs of onyx, 7 feet, 7 inches long, 25 inches wide.
2. Onyx cane, value $40.
2. Lump of carbonate of copper, weight 5,695 lbs. from "Copper Queen" mine.
2. Petrified woods.

UTAH.

2 Specimens of topaz.
1. Collection of native gems.
1. Gold, silver, copper and lead ores. Salt, sulphur, asbestos. Rock crystal. Mica. Crystals of selenite.

WASHINGTON.

2. Painting of Mt. Rainer, valued at $500.
2. Block of coal weighing 22 tons.
1. Collection of ores, coal and coke.

---

1. Wyoming—Coal pyramid. Minerals of the state.
2. Idaho—Opal display. Specimens of ore.
2. California—Ores, minerals and marble.
2. South Dakota—Mineral pyramid. Gold and tin.
2. Wisconsin—Fountain. Marble, granite and ore.

MICHIGAN.

2. Lumps of copper weighing 8,500 and 6,000 lbs. respectively.
2. Pyramid of sheet copper.
1. Models of ore docks, mining machinery, mills, etc.

---

1. Ohio—Pavilion decorations.
1. Kentucky—Pavilion in coal.
2. Oregon—Gold washing machinery in operation. Nickel ore.
1. Pennsylvania—Working model of coal mine and breaker. Coal, ores and building stone.
2. Along the entire east wall of the building will be found machinery used in mining, among which are: Rock and ore breaker, weight 60,-000 lbs, capacity 125 tons per hour. Cambria Iron company's exhibit. Kelley steel converter, used in 1861 and 1862. Randolph & Clows sheet brass and copper and seamless tubes. Hoisting machine, "The Chicago."

GALLERY.

WEST SIDE.

1. Case of marbles and imitations of precious stones.
1. United States geological and geographical surveys.

1. Collection of rocks from Ward's Natural Science establishment, Rochester, N. Y.
1. Relief map of United States.
1. Collection of curious ores and stones.
2. Tiffany collection precious stones, cut and uncut, representing every known form and style of cutting.
1. Samples of ore from famous Comstock lode.
1. Fluorite in case.
2. Crystals and ores in cases.
3. Statue, "Silver Queen," from Aspen Colorado.
2. Fourteen cases of Nevada precious stones and rare minerals, property of E. G. Morrison.
1. Rhinestones and amber.
1. Column representing value in gold of Empire mine, Germany, in 1891.
1. German precious stones and ores.
2. Aluminum specimens.

SOUTH END.

2. Exhibit of American tin plate manufacturers.

EAST SIDE.

3. Copies of celebrated nuggets: "The Welcome," largest ever found; value, $41,883.
3. Meteorite weighing 1,015 lbs; fell in Arizona. Ward collection of meteorites.
2. Assay office model.
1. Phosphates, sulphates, silicates, carbonates and oxides in cases.
2. Model of H. C. Frick coke works at Connelsville, Pa.
1. United States technical exhibit of coal.
2. New Pedrara display of onyx from Lower California. Jewel case.
1. Vermont marble.
2. Rose garnet from Mexico.
2. Asbestos rock and products from great bed in Georgia, 250 feet wide, 1,000 feet long and 60 feet deep. Found in this form in no other mine in the world.
2. Checker board made of Sioux Valley stone.

2. Standard Oil company exhibit of petroleum products.

ELECTRICITY BUILDING.

Dimensions, 345x690 feet. Cost, $401,000.

MAIN FLOOR.

1. Bell Telephone company's palace showing telephone exchange in operation. Case of apparatus showing evolution of the telephone.
1. Brush Electric Light company's motors.
1. Ft. Wayne Electric company's mammoth motors, generators and railway appliances.
1. Western Electric company's exhibit of underground wire system. "Egyptian Palace of Light."
1. Thomson electric light apparatus.
1. Westinghouse electric palace.
1. Latest electric light appliances from Frankfort on the Main.
2. Miniature electric railway in operation.
2. Key which President Cleveland pressed in starting the machinery of the World's Fair.
1. Queen & Co.'s university electric apparatus.
1. French exhibit of huge revolving bulls-eye prismatic lights.
1. Ringler's electrotyping works.
2. Tower of light.

GALLERY.

1. Model of German electric railway in operation.
2. Booth showing working of Mackay-Bennett cable system.
1. Engraving by electricity.

2. First phonograph made by Edison's employes.
1. Latest style phonograph.
2. Edison's latest invention, "the kinetograph," for taking instantaneous pictures.
1. German system by means of which anyone can operate the telegraph instrument.
1. Electric ball signal tower.
3. Wonderful German clock.

MACHINERY HALL.

Dimensions, 492x342 feet, with annex 490x550 feet. Floor area of both, 23.7 acres. Total cost, $1,200,000.

2. Power plant, largest in the world, supplying 24,000 horse power, of which 17,000 is devoted to electricity.
2. Boiler house, south side of hall.

SECTION C.

2. Electrical generator, 1,200 horse power.
1. Quadruple expansion engine, 2,000 horse power.
2. Westinghouse alternating current dynamos, 20,000 incandescent lights.

ANNEX.

1. Paper machine (Sec. A).
1. Severance nail cutting machine (Sec. A).
1. Saws, wood carving machine, box nailing machine (Sec. F).
1. Looms weaving silk in figures (Sec. O).
2. Electrical carpet sewing machine (Sec. N).
1. Printing and folding machines (Sec. P).

AGRICULTURAL BUILDING.

Dimensions, 800x500 feet, with annex 550x312 feet. Total cost, $620,000.

MAIN BUILDING.

SECTION A—N. E. QUARTER BUILDING.

1. The Netherlands—Cocoa, chocolate and drugs.
1. Sweden—Wood pulp and revolving stand.
1. Denmark—Curious shoes; agricultural products.
2. France—Agricultural products.
3. Menier chocolate tower; weight 50 tons, worth $40,000; made in one day.
1. Uruguay—Fertilizers and products.
2. Cape of Good Hope—Elephant tusk 7½ feet long, weight 160 lbs. Living Zulu boy 6 feet, 7½ inches tall. Head dress of Zulu chief. Wool, woods, ostrich feathers, skins. Stuffed ostrich and young.
2. New South Wales—Extensive display of wools.
2. Canada—Cheese weighing 22,000 pounds. Representation of Agricultural college. Farm products.
1. English exhibit.
1. Ceylon—Tea and coffee, from plant to cup. Tea valued at $175 per pound.
1. Model of Brookfield stud with pictures of famous horses.
2. Model of Hawarden castle, Gladstone estate.

SECTION B—N. W. QUARTER.

1. German exhibit. "Germania" in chocolate.
1. Spanish exhibit.
1. Brazil exhibit.
1. Brewing machinery.
1. Paraguay—Medicinal woods and plants. Tobacco, skins and snakes.
1. Ecuador.
2. British Guiana—Curiosities, minerals. Pyra-

mid representing gold product for term of years. Indian bread. 26 kinds of wood.
1. Japan—Tea industry.
1. Mexico.

SECTION C—S. E. QUARTER.

1. New York.
1. Missouri—Fine elk head. antlers in the velvet. Model of Eades bridge at St. Louis in reeds.
1. Washington.
1. Ohio—Display of tobacco.
1. Illinois—Display all products of state.
1. Pennsylvania—Artistic design Liberty Bell in cereals, hung in tower of grain and grasses.
1. Wyoming,
1. Colorado.

SECTION D—S. W. QUARTER.

2. Iowa—Corn palace, display of cereals and soil.
1. Nebraska.
1. Michigan.
1. Wisconsin—Booth made of native timber.
1. Montana.
1. North Dakota.
1. Maine—Native grasses and great variety of beans.
2. New Hampshire—Curious plow made and used by Daniel Webster. Typical New England corn crib enclosed in chestnut fence.
1. Oklahoma—Corn, cotton, sorghum.
1. Connecticut—Old-fashioned spinning wheel, table, etc.
1. Massachusetts.
1. French Experimental School of Agriculture exhibit.
1. Packing house meat exhibits.

GALLERY.

1. Egyptian tobacco.
1. Monument in soap representing origin of American flag.
1. Beer brewing company exhibits.

ANNEX—South of main building.

1. Agricultural implements.

Manufactures and Liberal Arts Building.

Dimensions, 787x1687 feet.   Cost $1,500,000. Floor space, 44 acres.

The first floor of the building is divided into sections. The main or "Columbian" aisle runs from north to south through the centre of the building. On the west side of this aisle are Sections A, B, C, D, E, F, G and H. On the east side are Sections I, K, L, M, N, O, P and Q. The visitor should begin at the south entrance and go north along the west side of the Columbian aisle, beginning with section A; then return to the south entrance and go north along the east side, beginning with section I. These tiers of sections extend from the Columbian aisle to the walls of the east and west sides, respectively, and are separated by small aisles running east and west. There are sub-divisions, but to avoid confusion only the sections will be used here to locate the exhibits enumerated. The section letters will be found on rows of posts running north and south through the building.

WEST SIDE—Section A.

ITALY.

2. Two majolica painting in front of pavilion, valued at $20,000 each.
2. "The Lion and his Prey," in bronze at entrance.
3. Remarkable collection of statuary in marble and bronze.
3. Florentine mosaics.
2. Statuary and carving in wood; 500 pieces.
1. Figures in gilt.

3. Lace worth $1,000 per yard. Brocades and tapestry.
1. Mirrors in curious shapes.
2. Pottery and glassware.

SPAIN.

2. Pavilion is a reproduction of Moorish Cathedral at Cordova, built between 1200 and 1214. The Spanish exhibit had not been opened when this book was printed. It should be inspected by every visitor. A part of this exhibit will be found in Section B.

PERSIA AND MEXICO.

2. Exhibits not in place when this book was printed. Many curious and rare articles will be found in each.

SIAM.

2. Pavilion is a model of a Siamese palace.
1. Elephant tusks 9 feet long.
(Not complete at this time.)

Section B.

BRAZIL.

1. Costumes of natives.
3. Collection of mosaics.
2. Collection of precious stones.
1. Furniture made in Brazil.
(Not complete at this time.)

HOLLAND.

2. Decorated wood imitations.
1. Small scales.

THE NETHERLANDS.

2. Decorated earthenware of many kinds.

SWITZERLAND.

2. Wood carving.
1. Scientific instruments.
2. Watches of every description.

DENMARK.

2. Delayed by ice blockade. Not open at this time.

ARGENTINE REPUBLIC.

2. Not open at this time.

MARSHALL FIELD'S EXHIBIT.

1. Handsome floor.
1. Curtains, rugs and other goods.

MONACO.

1. Ware and pottery.
3. Vase owned by the Pope. Took 4 years to make it; only one other like it in the world.

Section C.

CANADA.

1. Brick.
1. Steel saws.
2. Production by clock work of hair on baldheaded man and bangs on bangless woman.
1. Corticelli silk exhibit.
1. Musical instruments.
1. Work by pupils of Indian school.
1. Indian curiosities.

NEW SOUTH WALES.

1. Reversible card holder for window sash.
1. Leather.
1. Furniture.

EAST INDIA.

1. Hand work on fabrics.
2. Hand carved centre table, value $500; took three years to make.
3. Hindoo idols—very old.
2. Carving in ivory.
2. Hand carved writing desk.
2. Hand carved chair for lady.
2. Inlaid ivory cupboard.
3. Hand cutting and carving on metal.

2. Complete East India room. made of carved teakwood.
1. Antique candlestick valued at $150.
1. Teakwood bracket. valued at $250.
1. Carved teakwood chairs and tables.
2. East India swinging cradle

CEYLON

1. Fine tea and coffee.
1. Jugglery.
1. Twenty kinds of wood.
1. Native curiosities.

JAMAICA.

2. Inlaid wood table.
1. Rum.
2. Glass case containing many native curiosities and beautiful specimens of work by women of Jamaica.
1. Exhibit of 32 kinds of wood.

Section D

GREAT BRITAIN

2. Harry Hems & Sons—Wood sculpture. Christ on the cross
1. White & Sons—Display of pipes
1. Stanforth's exhibit of cutlery.
1. Brass bed 15 feet high and draped bed.
1. Moor Bros.—Decorated and fancy china ware.
1. John Wells.—Case of silverware containing crown worn by H. R. H. the late Duke of Essex.
   In the exhibit of A. B. Daniell & Son will be found the following:
2. China desert service used by Queen Victoria.
2. Sculptured glass.
2. Companion vases. representing "Strength" and "Beauty."
2. Vase, "Landing of Cupid's Crew."
2. Reproduction of famous Jubilee vase presented to Queen Victoria.
1. Reproduction of Senra spode porcelain,

1. Service used by Count Airlie in 1784.
1. Reproduction of ware of 1793.
   In Goldsmith and Silversmith Mfg. Exhibit.
2. Columbus shield of silver.
3. Columbus clock showing time at Greenwich, Madrid, Paris and Chicago.
2. Gladstone casket.
1. Wosterholm & Son—Big knife.
1. Joseph Gillott's exhibit of pens.
1. Sunlight Soap pavilion.
1. Burroughs & Wellion—Case of surgical instruments carried by Stanley in African explorations.
1. Madame Kate Reily—Wedding gowns.
1. Gregory & Co.—Holbem sideboard of Italian walnut.
1. Wm. Wallman—Copper used as wall paper. Leather paper. Embossed paper.
2. Doulton & Co.—Historical vase. Columbia vase. Collection of vases.
3. Arup Bros.—Terra cotta statuary.
1. Brown, Whitehead, Moore & Co. —Cauldon chinaware.
2. Hampton & Sons—Reproduction of banquet hall in Hatfield House, the historical seat of the Marquis of Salisbury.
2. Royal Porcelain Works—Complete table set. Russet table set. Richly jeweled vases. Plates of elegant design.

Section E.

2. Columbian clock and tower in exact centre of building.

GERMANY.

2. Pavilion and fountain.
3. Costly shields, plates, tankards, etc., gifts of honor to the Emperors, and to Bismark and VonMoltke.
3. Furniture from a room in the palace of the King of Bavaria.

2. Bavarian Art Industry Association of Munich, including 135 exhibitors and showing 8 rooms furnished in style of 8 epochs.
2. Royal Saxon porcelain exhibit. Large pictures in porcelain.
1. Saxon laces and cloths.
2. Painting of Nuremberg market place.
3. Heroic bronze group, "Germania," for German parliament building; loaned by the Emperor.
1. Arts objects embossed in copper, by H. Seitz.
1. Exhibit of chemicals, drugs, etc., from 72 firms.
1. Stationery and paper products, photogravures, etc.
2. Illustration of manufacture of paper from cellular products.
1. Iron enamel exhibit.
1. Fine art metal goods.
2. Henkel's cutlery.
2. Embossed leather goods. Handwork.
2. Royal Porcelain Manufactory of Berlin.
1. Great wrought iron gates, hand-made.
1. Ecclesiastical exhibit—Stained windows, carvings and statuettes.
2. Christ's Descent From the Cross.
1. Collective exhibit of clocks and watches. Cuckoo and musical clocks. Oberammergau clock.
1. Silk and satin fabrics, laces and embroideries.
2. The Sonneberg toy industries.
1. Porcelain, majolica and iron ranges.

Section F.

AUSTRIA.

3. Fac-simile of salon of the Duchess of Metternich.
2. Portrait of the Emperor woven in silk.
2. Albums belonging to the imperial family.
3. Gifts of honor to the Emperor—vases, jewels, etc., in case.
1. Collective turnery exhibit by 35 Vienna manufacturers in amber and meerschaum, pearl, metal, ivory and wood.

2. Collective exhibit of porcelain, majolica, Faience and Bohemian glassware.
2. Fac-similes of bronzes made for the Emperor.
2. Waschman exhibit of chiseled, embossed, bronze, silver and leather goods.
2. Hand decorated porcelain exhibit of E. Wahliss.
1. Terra cotta.
2. Large porcelain vases at portal; valve $2,000.
1. Publishers' display of art books, photogravures, etc.

Section G.

JAPAN.

1. Exhibits of toilet articles, chemicals, etc.
1. Fireworks and joss sticks.
1. Unique exhibit of papers. Process of making paper articles shown. Bleached bark of Papyrifera, from which paper is made.
2. Great variety of lacquer work and process shown. Inlaid work.
2. Yuzeen screens and hangings for decorative purposes.
3. Three mammoth Cloisonne vases, valued at $50,000.
1. Exhibits of china, art metal work, carved slate ware, wood and ivory carving, porcelain sculpture, bamboo incised work.
1. Raw silk and silk fabrics.
2. Fac-simile of Japanese house and interior of parlor, with furnishings and decorations.
1. Picture of rice planting.
2. Four vases 300 years old.
2. Vases with all kinds of porcelain work represented thereon.
2. Japanese robes and embroidered screens, fans and artificial flowers.
1. Lanterns and candlesticks.
1. Metal statues and incense burners.
2. Temple bell tower.
2. Massive silver punch bowl and other articles made by S. Ogeki.

3. Iron eagle. This figure is 2 feet in height, and spread of wings from tip to tip is 5 feet; weight, 133 pounds. The head moves freely, like that of a living bird. There are more than 3,000 feathers, each of which was made separately by hand. The lines on the feathers may be counted by hundreds, on some of them by thousands. These lines were made by a sharp tool, which had to be replaced every third or fourth line in order that lines might be uniform. The maker procured two eagles, one of which he killed and stuffed and the other he kept alive in order to observe its movements. It required five years continuous labor to complete the work.
2. Exhibit from Kioto, including embroidery, fabrics, silks and porcelain.

Section H.

1. Exhibit of granite and marble industries of Vermont.
2. Model of Volk's heroic statue of Lincoln. Model of colossal staute of Columbus recently erected in Chicago.
1. Mosaics and ceramics.
1. Pottery and earthenware.
1. Gunther's fur exhibit—75 stuffed and mounted animals.

EAST SIDE—Section I.

1. Musical instruments—Pipe organs, brass instruments, harps, drums, silver horns, violins, mandolins and banjos.
2. M. Steinert's collection of ancient keyed and string instruments.
1. Pilcher's tubular pneumatic pipe organ.
1. Pianos of all styles.

Section K.
NORWAY.

1. Mountain scenery. Model cottage. Costumes.

Fur and stuffed animals. Milk condensing apparatus.
1. Sledges. Wood carvings. Canoes.
1. Wines and liqnors.
1. Unbleached bi-sulphide pulp.

RUSSIA.

3. Pottery and ware from the Czar's collection.
1. Fabrics and tapestries.
1. Press exhibit.
2. Government papers.
1. Costumes of the people.
3. Furs.
(Incomplete at this time.)

CHINA.

1. Shewan & Co.'s teas, silks and cassia house.
1. Models of Chinese street scenes.
1. Tea drinking booth.
1. Lee Kewong Kee company's teas, meats and fnrs.
1. Chinese pagoda.
(Incomplete at this time.)

Section L.

BELGIUM.

2. Twelve-fronted bronze vase ornamented in colors, made by a process which is now a lost art.
2. Statue, " Leonidas at Thermopylae."
2. Statue, " Innocence Troubled by the Loves," a Florentine bronze.
2. Elegant vases, placques and pottery of Boch Bros.
2. Case of rare laces and fans from Brussels.
1. Paintings of the city of Ostend.
1. Pottery and china.
1. Tapestries.
1. Case of costly lamps and stands.
1. Zinc palace.
1. Statuary made of cement by new process.
1. Case of birds.
1. Old Belgian stoves.

Section M.

FRANCE.

This exhibit covers also part of Section L. Not complete at this time.

2. Bronze statuary and armory.
2. Glarnger vases, value $2,500 each
2. Christofle's silver and bronzes.
1. Egyptian wares.
1. Leon Henry's china and pottery.
3. Cabinet, value, $25,000.
2. Electric candelabras, value, $7,500.
2. Susse Freres bronzes —Defence of the Flag, value, $6,000. Song of Departure, value, $6,000. The Dance, $600. Summer, $500. Mignon.
3. The celebrated Dore vase.
3. Leblanc-Barbedienne bronze and silverware. Bronzed ebony cabinet, value, $13,000. Cabinet, enameled panels, value, $5,000. Casket value, $6,000. Statue of Cæsar.
1. Glarnzer's clocks.
1. Blots Statuary and bronzes.
1. Pindedo's bronzes.
1. Duval's bronzes and brasses.
1. Harmot-Poivier tapestry and furniture booth.
1. Tapestry palace.
1. French dolls.
1. Bricard Bros.' brasses.
1. Millet's tapestry and furnishings.
1. Gagnean lamps.

Section N.

2. Tiffany gold and silver palace, containing wares valued at $500,000. Diamonds. Gold and silver ingots. Precious stones. Gold and Silver plate.
2. Tiffany stained glasses.
2. Meriden Britannia company's mahogany and plate glass palace, containing gold and silver ware valued at $400,000.
1. Rogers Bros.' spoons and self-winding clocks.
1. Wm. Rogers' silverware booth.

1. Pierpont Mfg. company's white palace containing precious wares.
2. Gorham Mfg. Co., "Silver Smith's Palace."
1. Designs for stained glass windows and ceramics.
1. Benziger Bros.' brass and silver.
1. Rockwood pottery.
1. Bedstead exhibit.
1. Klaber's marble palace.
1. Vallrath's enameled iron.
1. Wallpaper palace.
1. Mermod & Jaccard (jewelry) palace, typical of Louis' of France, decorated in fleur de lis and rocco work.
1. Lind's exhibit of jewelry.

———

Section O.

2. Waltham exhibit of 2,000 watches. Machines making watches.
2. Waltham's old sun dial, 1630.
3. Waterbury Watch company's "Century" clock; cost $80,000 and was 10 years in construction, every piece being carved out by hand. In different sections of this clock are miniature workshops in operation, showing all inventions since Whitney's cotton gin.
1. Keystone Watch company's exhibit — Silver watch case weighing 5 lbs. 7 oz.
1. Cheney Bros.' changeable silks.
3. Locomotive made of Belding Bros.' spool silk.
1. Silk gloves. Columbian souvenir ribbons. Silk dresses.
1. Carpen's upholstered furniture.
1. Spool silk exhibit.

———

Section P.

1. Woolen goods.
1. Cashmeres.
1. Vaults and safes.
1. Tools and cutlery.

Section Q.

1. Gatling guns.
1. Smith & Wesson revolver, valued at $350.
1. Remington, Colt and Winchester fire-arms.
3. Arizona petrified forest.
1. Brunswick-Balke-Calender company's elephant tusks.
1. Roebling's wire cables.
2. "Sapolio." The small boat 14 feet 6 inches long in which Captain Andrews crossed the ocean.
1. Pennsylvania Salt company's huge block of crystal alum made from Greenland kryolite; weight 12 tons.
1. Lindbourg's silver statuary.

GALLERY.

The gallery is also divided into sections, distinguished by letters on posts. On the west side are Sections A, B, C and D; on the north end, Section E; on the east side Sections F, G, H and I; on the south end, Section K. The visitor should begin at the southwest corner of the gallery and, going north, make the complete circuit to the point from whence he started. As on the first floor, subdivisions and figures are not used in locating the following exhibits, as they tend to confuse the observer. The main sections have aisles through them, running east and west.

WEST SIDE—Section A.

1. Exhibit of Spanish educational institutions.
1. Educational exhibits, as follows: Florida High schools. Pratt Institute of New York. Pennsylvania schools. New Jersey schools. South Dakota schcols. Minnesota schools. Nebraska schools. Philadelphia educational exbibit. American Institute for Feeble Minded. New York Cooper Union Art exhibit. Art Student's League of New York. State Institutions for the Blind. Iowa schools.
1. Paintings from Museum of Fine Arts, Boston.

1. Minneapolis School of Fine Arts.
1. Chinese school exhibit—model of pagoda, maps and chemical apparatus.
1. St. Louis School of Fine arts.
1. Colorado schools exhibit. Model of Indian camp. Model of first school house built in Colorado.
1. German photographic art.
1. Russian educational exhibit.
1. German photo-ceramics.
1. Russian art exhibit.

Section B.

2. New South Wales school exhibit—Scenes in Australia. Birds. Australian curiosities. Drawings. Fancy work.
2. Canadian schools—Curiosities from the monastery of Ursulines at Quebec. Mt. St. Louis exhibit of curios and ancient manuscripts.
1. St. Thomas art and school exhibit.
1. Waterlow & Son's exhibit of postage stamps and curios.
2. London exhibit of old newspapers of every description from the date of invention of printing.
1. London school exhibit.
1. South Kensington art exh'bit.
1. Oxford University Extension exhibit.
1. Raphael Tuck & Sons' color paintings.
2. Vanderveydes photographic exhibit — The Prince of Wales. "Hypatia."
1. Lafayette's (London) photographs of noted people.
2. Photographic Loan collection from England.
1. Werner & Sons' (Dublin) photographs.

Section C.

1. German glassware.
1. German educational exhibit. Photographs of universities. Electrical educational appliances of recent invention. Chemical apparatus. Incubators for hatching microbes.

1. Orchestral organ. Music box, valued at $1,500. Orchestral organs from Berlin.
2. Oil painting of Alexander Von Humboldt.
1. Rare manuscripts of Goethe and other German poets and scholars.
1. German tapestry.
1. Case showing evolution in hats from 1350 to 1893.

Section D.

1. Milanese armor.
1. Society of Christian Endeavor exhibit.
1. Bureau of the Peace Societies of the World exhibit.
1. Y. M. C. A. exhibit.
1. Exhibit of bibles.
1. Statuary typical of the city of Vienna

Section E—North End.

THE ''CENTURY'' BOOTH.

2. Manuscript of Lincoln's inaugural address.
2. Original draft of the proclamation calling out the first 75,000 militia, April 15, 1861.
2. Lincoln's bill for his first surveying.
2. Lincoln's answer to a challenge from Brig. Gen. James Shields.
1. Manuscript of Lincoln's speech on presenting Gen. Grant with his command.
2. Lincoln's manuscripts and material used in "Century" history by Nicolay and Hay.
2. Manuscript of proclamation of amnesty to states.
2. Jefferson Davis' letter to Lincoln.
2. Lincoln's letters to generals.
1. Manuscript of first chapter of '' Little Lord Fauntleroy.''
1. Correspondence of Gen. Sherman and Senator John Sherman.
1. Manuscripts of letters used in the "Century" war pap ers.
2. Pencil used by Lee in signing surrender to Grant.
1. Case illustrating process of wood engraving and photo half-tone process.

1. Original of James Whitcomb Riley's poem, "Little Wesley."
1. Manuscripts of stories by Frank R. Stockton, W. D. Howells, Charles Dudley Warner, Henry James, H. C. Bunner. Joel Chandler Harris, Bret Harte, J. G. Holland, T. B. Aldrich, Geo. W. Cable and others.
1. Autograph letters of Lowell and Holland.
1. Original drawings of illustrations in "War Papers."
2. First copy of Garrison's *National Philanthropist*.
1. Last words of original manuscript of Frank R. Stockton's "The Lady or the Tiger."
2. Piece of wooden book cover used by George Kennan to conceal his manuscript in Siberia.
1. Original drawings made by Mr. Frost in Siberia for the Kennan papers.
1. Exhibit of old dictionaries from 1616 to 1893.
1. Manuscripts of Longfellow, Tennyson, Whittier and other poets.

CHARLES SCRIBNER'S SONS' EXHIBIT.

2. First edition of Vicar of Wakefield.
1. Rare editions of Keats, Shelley, Horace and other poets.
1. Manuscripts in full of May number of Scribner's magazine.
1. Manuscripts of celebrated novelists.

EAST SIDE.

As many of the exhibits extend through more than one section on this side of the gallery, the sections are not named in describing them. The visitor will find the following in order as he proceeds south:

1. Chicago manufacturers' exhibit of stained glass.
1. Rawson and Evans, ornamental glass.
1. Edison mimeographs.
1. California wood novelties. Tree bark pin cushions.
1. Tannette—a substitute for leather.
1. Goodyear hard rubber specialties.

1. Cleveland and his cabinet in wax.
1. Foster kid glove exhibit in gold finish case.
1. Sewing machine manufacturers' exhibit.
1. Demuth & Co's pipes.

FRENCH EXHIBIT.

Incomplete at this time.

1. Photographs, lithographs and chromos.
1. French fashion plates (ladies) from 1840 to 1893, in colors.
2. Fac-similes of famous French paintings and etchings.
1. Catholic educational exhibits.
1. Indian Industrial School (Carlisle, Pa.) exhibit.
1. Public and Normal school exhibits.
1. Wilberforce University (colored) exhibit.

SOUTH END.

2. Exhibits from leading colleges and art and industrial schools of the United States.

GOVERNMENT BUILDING.

Dimensions, 345x415 feet.   Cost $400,000.

The several departments of the U. S. Government occupy space in this building. The name of each department will be found in large letters over the space occupied, and the visitor will have no difficulty in finding the exhibits listed under this head.

SMITHSONIAN INSTITUTE.

1. Specimens of bones of men, birds and animals.
1. Case of fine specimens of domestic fowls, stuffed and mounted; among them the cele-

brated Indian Game cock "Agitator;" also, fine specimens of Langshan, Black Java, Light Brahma, Exhibition Game, Cochin and Hamburg fowls.

1. Pigeon house and pigeons of all noted varieties.
1. Reproduction of wild turkey pen and trap.
2. Flamingoes, nests and eggs.
1. Specimens of birds showing variations according to locality.
2. Case of humming birds, showing 183 different kinds.
2. Case of Birds of Paradise.
2. Case containing 1,400 specimens, representing 106 families of American birds.
2. Case of pheasants and jungle fowls, among them the *Gallus Bankivd*, or jungle fowl of India, from which nearly all domestic fowls have sprung.
1. Lyre kite of prairie.
1. Carolina paroquets roosting and feeding.
1. Case representing grouse, partridge and turkey families.
1. Butcher bird and nest.
1. California woodpecker.
2. Bower bird and playhouse which it constructs —only bird that builds both nest and playhouse.
1. Ptarmidgeons in protective colors—white in winter, brown in summer.
1. Owls—largest and smallest.
1. Chinese, Mongolian and Impeyan pheasants.
1. Harpy—largest eagle known.
2. Condor—very large specimen.
1. Honduras turkey.
1. Screamers.
1. English thrush, nest and young.
1. California buzzard.
1. Sonnerat's jungle fowl.
1. Courtship of prairie chickens illustrated.
2. Rocky Mountain goats, standing on rocky crags, Montana
1. Rocky Mountain sheep.
1. Barren ground caribou of Alaska.

1. Woodland caribou of Newfoundland.
1. Group of badgers.
1. Group of armadillos from Texas.
3. Sea otter, mounted on rock; fur most valuable in the world, one skin bringing from $300 to $500.
1. American bison.
1. Sacred ox of India.
1. Wood rats and nest.
3. Pacific walrus, finest specimen ever exhibited.
2. Group California sea lions.
1. Group Virginia opposum.
2. Representation of every family of mammals in North and South America.
2. Collection illustrating commercial use of skins, feathers, hair, wool and bones of animals.
2. Tiffany collection of 300 kinds of leather.
1. Utilization of hoofs and hair.
1. Teeth of animals and manufactured products.
1. Ivory from elephant and norwhal.
1. Implements made of bone.
2. Crocodile of the Nile and crocodile birds, showing birds feeding from mouth of crocodile.
1. Group of Virginia deer.
1. Specimens of fishes and reptiles in alcohol.
1. Collection of portraits of men prominent in various fields of research in America.
1. Extensive collection of coins and metals.
2. Harris collection.
1. Case showing chemical construction and composition of parts of human body.

ETHNOLOGY.

1. Figures of Esquimaux and specimens of their art and industry.
1. Canadian Indians, arts and products.
1. Indian tepee.
1. Figures of Indians of the plains.
1. Pacific coast Indian.
1. Chippewa Indian.
1. Representative Crow Indian.
1. Collection Southern California Indian arts and industries.

1. Sioux Indian tanning hides.
1. Zuni Indian.
1. Ute Indian.
2. Representation of prehistoric American.
2. Comparative industries of different ages of Europe and America, represented by stone implements.
1. Rudest stone implements of the American savage.
1. Stone cutters art among Indians of North America at time of discovery by Columbus.
1. Ancient pottery.
2. Models of ruins in Arizona, the most extensive ruins in America.
1. Apache and Comanche boys in hunting costume.
1. Indian from extreme south.

LIMESTONE CAVERN PHENOMENA.

1. Products of caves.
1. Animal life in caves.
1. Illustration of process of formation of stalactites, showing time required.
2. Piece of roof and part of floor from Marengo cave, Indiana.
1. Photographs of cave interior.

VOLCANIC AND GLACIAL.

1. Model of ice spring craters near Fillmore, Utah.
1. Specimen of volcanic phenomena.
1. Photograph of Bogoslof volcano in action.
1. Boulders from glacial drifts.
2. Piece of limestone planed by glacier.
1. Photograph of boulders.
2. Map representing United States during glacial period.

MINERAL.

2. Collection of gems of the United States.
1. Specimens of lapidary work.
2. Mineral specimens illustrating colors.

ANTIQUITIES.

This collection is in the southwest corner of the building.

1. Collection of old musical instruments—brass, wind and string.
1. Indian curiosities.
1. Embroidery representing Elijah fed by the ravens.
1. Tapestry representing story of David and Bathsheba.
3. Brass lamp used at the feast of the dedication of Hunneikah, B. C., 169.
1. Scrolls of the law of Tarah, made in Asia Minor in 10th century.
1. Manuscript copy of Book of Esther.
1. Embroidery representing defeat of Goliath.
3. Linen table center used at Passover meal.
3. Embroidery used to cover dish of greens at Passover meal.
1. Silver spice box of time of Christ.
3. Brass dish used at Passover meal.
1. Knife and cup used at rite of circumcision.
1. Phylacteries or Tefflin used by the Jews at morning prayers, except on Saturdays.
3. Twelve wine glasses used at Passover meal
1. Hebrew Pentateuch.
1. Jewish prayerbooks.
1. Knife used by priests in slaying animals for sacrifice.
1. Koran stand inlaid with mother of pearl.
2. Statuary representing progress of Christianity by epochs.

STATE DEPARTMENT.

3. Original manuscript of Declaration of Independence.
3. Original petition of United Colonies to George III, presented by Benjamin Franklin in 1774.
3. Gen. Jackson's sword.
2. Original journal of the Continental Congress.
2. Lincoln's Emancipation Proclamation.
1. Portraits of American statesmen.
1. Autograph letter of George III.
1. Proclamations of presidents with autographs.
2. Letters written by Washington, Franklin, the

Adamses, Jefferson, Madison, Jackson, Polk, Van Buren, Monroe, Lincoln, Grant, Arthur and Hayes.

2. Punch bowl presented by Washington to Col. Eyre.
2. Treaty with Napoleon for cession of Louisiana.
1. The Webster-Ashburton treaty, signed by Queen Victoria.
1. Shark's tooth sent as a treaty by the King of Samoa.
1. Credentials of Chinese minister.
2. Letters written by Napoleon, Alexander of Russia and other European potentates.

GALLERY.

2. Pictures and specimens from Mexico, Central America and South America.

UNDER DOME.

In cases and on the walls around the circle under the dome are Revolutionary and Colonial relics contributed by the ladies of the several states. This exhibit is not under the control of the State Department, but may be properly described under that head.

3. Washington's commission as commander in chief of Colonial forces.
3. Washington's sword.
3. Washington's diary, account books, and army reports.
3. Sash used by Lafayette to bind up his wound at the battle of Brandywine.
3. Calumet pipe smoked by Washington at 17.
3 Benjamin Franklin's cane.
3. Waistcoat embroidered by Queen Marie Antoinette.
2. Wampum made before discovery of America.
3. Camp service of pewter used by Washington throughout the Revolution.
2. Bible brought over in the Mayflower by John Alden in 1620.
3. Part of the torch carried into the wolf's den by "Old Put" (General Israel Putnam).

THE "BIG TREE."

3. In the center of the space under the dome is a section of one of the great trees of California It is 26 feet in diameter at the base and 20 feet in diameter at the top. and has been hollowed out and has a stairway within.

DEPARTMENT OF JUSTICE.

2. Warrant for arrest and imprisonment for debt, issued in reign of George I. 1721.
2. Page from Plymouth records of 1620 and 1621.
2. Land Patent issued in 1628.
2 Commission of William III. creating common pleas court of Massachusetts in 1695.
2. Agreement in regard to enlarging Salem church. 1638.
2. Page of record of wit hcraft trial in 1692 and report of examination of witnesses.
3. Earliest charter of free government known to man—the Compact of Providence.
1. Fac-simile of Penn's charter.
2. Door-knocker that came in the Mayflower
1. Portraits of Justices and Attorney Generals of the Supreme Court of the United States.

WAR DEPARTMENT.

1. Engineering department—river and harbor improvement. machinery, models and plans.
1. Fish torpedo.
2. Six-pounder bronze gun presented to Colonial forces by Lafayette.
2. Cartridge making machinery in operation.
3. Four-pounder gun that fired the first shot of the Rebellion.
3. Rifled gun that fired the last shot of the Rebellion.
1. Cannon used in Mexican war.
1. Cast iron cannon found in Hudson river—very old.
1. Chinese cannon captured in Corea.
2. Bronze cannon captured at Yorktown.

1. Blanchard lathe—oldest in existence.
3 Arctic scene representing Greeley welcoming return of Lockwood.
3. Flag displayed at point nearest North Pole.
2. Painting of Lockwood at farthest point North.
2. Masonic flag displayed by Greeley at farthest point North.
1. Boot-legs from which soup was made by Greeley party when out of provisions.
1. Signal service instruments.
2. Relics of Sir John Franklin discovered by Schwatka; his hair.
1. Arlington National Cemetery in miniature.
2. Modern 52 ton, 12 inch gun, 37 feet long. Weight of projectile, 1,000 lbs; charge of powder, 450 lbs.
1. Eight inch coast defense gun : projectile, 300 lbs ; charge, 130 lbs.
2. Maxim gun, capacity, 650 to 700 shots per minute.
1. Veterinary exhibit.
1. Wagon that was in Sherman's train through all his marches.
1. Indian Relics—sacred shirt worn by Sitting Bull in fight where Custer was killed.
1. Figures of officers and soldiers in Revolutionary uniform.
1. Figures of officers and soldiers in uniform of 1812.

TREASURY DEPARTMENT.
3. U. S. Mint in operation.
1. Collection of historical medals.
1. Coins of the United States, Mexico, Canada and South America.
2. Collection of ancient coins.
1. U. S. Bonds, Colonial bills and old currency.
1. Ten thousand dollar gold certificate.
1. Ten thousand dollar silver certificate.
1. Collection of old bills in case.
1. Model of first order light house.
1. Model of light house, Minot's ledge.
1. Government telescopes and chronographs.

POSTOFFICE DEPARTMENT.

1. Postage stamps of the United States from 1847 to 1893.
2. Collection of Dead Letter Office curiosities.
1. Locks used in U. S. Mail service, 1800 to 1893.
1. Rocky Mountain mail coach built in 1868.
1. Dogs drawing sled with U. S. mail.
1. World's Fair postoffice.

PATENT OFFICE.

This department is devoted to exhibits of models of inventions that have been patented. In the annex will be found an interesting exhibit of plows, showing the improvements made during several centuries.

INTERIOR DEPARTMENT.

1. Globe 20 feet in diameter.
1. Pictures of schools and school buildings.
1. Bureau of education and educational statistics of the U. S. and other countries.
2. Mechanical schedule of time used in the University of Kansas.
1. Models of school house furniture.
2. Collection of work by native pupils in Alaska.
1. Electric tabulating machines.

GEOLOGICAL SURVEY.

1. Geological relief maps.
1. Collection of shells.
1. Leaf and insect formation on rocks.
1. Collection of geological specimens in cases.
1. Surveying instruments.
2. Skeleton democerta order of mammals.

AGRICULTURAL DEPARTMENT.

1. Forestry specimens.
2. Lanterns of wood vaneer.
1. Wood saving appliances.
1. Collection of American plants and grasses.
2. Artificial American fruits.
1. Collection of insects in cases.

1. Fungus diseases of plants.
1. Animals injurious and beneficial to agriculture.
1. Exhibit showing distribution of animals according to elevation.
1. Model of life zones.
1. Fungi exhibit.
1. Agricultural Statistical exhibit.
2. Illustration of tagging cattle for export.
1. Working laboratory and study of diseases.
1. Agricultural museum of exhibits.
1. Cereal exhibit.
1. Tobacco exhibit,
1. Wood and vegetable fibre.
1. Weather bureau exhibit.   ·
1. Metereological signs.

U. S. FISH COMMISSION

3. Fish hatching station, showing eggs of fish in
   process of hatching.
1. Shad and cod fishing and spawning.
1. Historical series of hatching apparatus.
1. Model of hatching station.
2. Deep sea sounding appliances and dredges.
2. Casts of all kinds of fish.
1. Group of sea lions and seals.
1. Fishing vessels.
2. Alaska fishing village in miniature.
2. Collection of anglers flies illustrated by Mrs.
   Mabay.
2. Representation of "Scientific Angler."
1. Rod and reel exhibit by Abbey & Imbrey
2. Representation of "Ideal Still Fisher."
1. Whaling boat apparatus.
1. Seal and walrus boat.
2. Alaskan fishing implements and applianc.es.
2. Water color paintings of Alaskan seal islands
   and scenery by H. W. Elliott.
1. Farrington exhibit of flies.
1. Deep sea specimens.
1. Casts of fish raised by U. S. Fish Commission.
2. Casts of whales, blackfishes, etc.
1. Alaskan boat carved from one log.
1. Ornamental American corals.

FINE ART BUILDING.

Dimensions, 320 x 500 feet with two annexes, each 120 x 200 feet. Cost, $670,000. It contains the finest collection ever exhibited.

GERMANY.

3. William I. Apotheosis.—Keller.
2. William II. Hunting Whales.—Saltzman.
1. Portrait of Mommsen.—Knaus.
1. Death of Dante.—Frederick.
1. Pope Leo XIII.—Leuback.
2. Battle of Orleans.—Adam.
2. A Martyr's Daughter.—Bauer.
2. Announcement of the Shepherds.--Uhde.
1. A Nun.—Hoecker.
1. The Last Chance.—Grethe.
3. William II.—Schuch.
3. Tullia.—Hildebrande.
2. Herod's daughter.--Papparitz.
2. Bavarian Tap.—Gabl.
2. Fishing in Norway.—Eckenaes.
1. Breakers.—Mueller.
2. Finding the Slain.—Meckel.
2. Fresh Water.—Braith.
2. Portrait of Kossuth.—Mme. Parlaghy.
1. Turlight.--Block.
2. An Amusing Chronicle. }
   A Good Hand.   } —Kronberger.
1. Pride of the Family.—Simm.

GREAT BRITAIN.

2. No. 57. A Dedication to Bacchus.—Alma Tadema.
2. No. 58. An Audience at Agrippa's.—Alma Tadema.
2. No. 59. The Sculpture Gallery.—Alma Tadema.

LOANED BY QUEEN VICTORIA.

3. No. 105. The Roll Call.—Lady Butler.
3. No. 121. Royal Jubilee Procession.—Charlton.
3. No. 321. Return From Plowing.—G. H. Mason.

LOANED BY THE PRINCE OF WALES.

3. No. 525. The Royal Yacht Squadron.—Sir Oswald Brierly.
3. No. 526. The Ocean Yacht Race.—Sir Oswald Brierly.

MISCELLANEOUS.

2. No. 138. Death of Cleopatra.—Hon. John Collier.
2. No. 139. Circe.—Hon. John Collier.
3. No. 143. Freedom.—Walter Crane.
2. No. 149. The Passing of Arthur.—Frank Dicksee.
2. No. 150. The Redemption of Tannhauser.—Frank Dicksee.
1. No. 197. Christ and the Magdalen.—Hacker.
2. No. 204 The Victory of Faith.—St. George Hare.
2. No. 93. "For of Such is the Kingdom of Heaven.—Bramley.
1. No. 113. Two Little Home Rulers.—Madam Canziani.
1. No. 122. Incident in Charge of Light Brigade.—Charlton.
1. No. 183. By the Sea of Galilee.—Goodall.
1. No. 193. Caledonia, Stern and Wild.—Graham.
1. No. 254. The Curse of the family.—Kennington.
1. No. 274. Hercules Wrestling with Death for the Body of Alcestes.—Sir Frederick Leighton.
2. No. 275. Garden of the Hesperides.—Sir Frederick Leighton.
2. No. 276. Perseus and Andromeda.—-Sir Frederick Leighton.
1. No. 288. The Benediction.—Sir James Linton.
1. No. 317. Pygmalion.—Margetson.

2.	No. 331.	The Ornithologist.—Sir John Millais.
2.	No. 332.	Halcyon Weather.—Sir John Millais.
2.	No. 333.	Last Rose of Summer.—Sir John Millais.
2.	No. 335.	Lingering Autumn.—Sir John Millais.
2.	No. 336.	Shelling Peas.—Sir John Millais.
1.	No. 352.	The River Road.—D. Murray.
1.	No. 398.	The Broken Idol.—Prinsep.
2.	No. 411.	Requiescat.—Riviere.
2.	No. 413.	The Magician's Doorway.—Riviere.
2.	No. 422.	EarlyChristians and Lions.—Schmalz.
1.	No. 486.	Love and Life.—Watts.
1.	No. 487.	Love and Death.—Watts.
1.	No. 518.	Calling theWorshipers.—Alma Tadema.
1.	No. 535 and 536.	Church and Refectory of Rievaulx Abbey.—Walter Crane.
1.	No. 619.	Departure of the Fleet.—Langley.

FRANCE.

3. Portraits of Renan and Cardinal Lavigene, by Bonnat, President of French Society of Artists.
3. Portrait of Pope Leo XIII, by Chartran, the only painter to whom the Pope has given a sitting.
2. The Snake Charmer.—Gerome.
2. A Street in Cairo —Gerome.
3. Christopher Columbus.—Benjamin Constant.
3. The Drought.—Benjamin Constant.
2. The Holy Women of the Sepulchre.—Bouguereau.
2. Our Lady of the Angels.—Bouguereau.
3. Pardon at Kergoat.—Jules Breton.
3. Young Girls Joining the Procession.—Jules Breton.
2. The Passing Regiment.—D'Etaille.
2. The Attack on Convoy.—D'Etaille.
2. The Descent from the Cross.—Bereaud.
3. Portrait of President Carnot, by Yoon.
1. Japan.—Louis Abbema.

2. Vanity.—Agache.
2. A Magician.—Agache.
2. The Annunciation.—Agache.
2. Morning on the Sea Shore.—Bertrand.
3. La Rouscoulade.—Rosa Bonheur.
3. King of the Forest.—Rosa Bonheur.
2. The Angler.—Gilbert.
2. A Fete at Tokio.—De Moulin.
2. Primitive Man.—Benner.
2. The Booty.—Rochegrosse.
2. The Fiancees.—Rochegrosse.
2. A Ball in 1830 (water color).—Madeleine Le-maire.
2. Adieu (water color).—Madeleine Lemaire.
3. Exhibit of medals and cameos.

AUSTRIA.

3. Nos. 70 to 74. The Five Senses.—Hans Makart.
2. No. 75. The Falconer. (Loaned by the Emperor)—Hans Makart.
2. No. 32. Children Playing with a Dog.—Franz Von Defregger.
2. No. 33. "God Bless You."—Franz Von Defregger.
2. No. 29. Master of the Hounds—Hans Canon.
2. No. 26. Fenstersturz.—V. Brocik.
2. No. 27. The First Communion of the Hussites.—V. Brocik.
2. No. 78. Market Place in Cairo.—L. C. Mueller.
2. No. 112. A Wolf.—Otto Thoren.
2. No. 97. "Let the Little Ones Come Unto Me."—Julius Schmid.
2. No. 88. Gipsy Hut.—August Pettenkofer.
1. No. 86. Market.—August Pettenkofer.
2. No. 69. Gulf of Quarnero.—E. Lichtenfels.
1. Nos. 83 and 84. Autumn Scenes.—Franz Pansinger.
2. No. 114. Morning at the Seashore.—Florian Wiesinger.
2. No 116. Laundress of the Mountains.—Florian Wiesinger.

HOLLAND.

2. No. 7. Girl Knitting.—D. A. C. Artz.
1. No. 8. The Pet Lamb.—D. A. C. Artz.
1. No. 10. Idle Hours in the Dunes.—D. A. C. Artz.
1. No. 9. Fall in the Fields.—D. A. C. Artz.
1. No. 32. Dutch Reformed Church in Haarlem.—J. Bosboon.
1. No. 33. Synagogue in Amsterdam.—J. Bosboon.
2. No. 108. Wood Carts.—Anton Mauve.
2. No. 109. Cows Going Home.—Anton Mauve.
2. No. 111. Ploughing.—Anton Mauve.
1. No. 94. The Two Mills.—J. Maris.
1. No. 97. Fishing Shells.—J. Maris.
1. No. 98. Canal at Rotterdam.—J. Maris.
2. No. 99. Under the Willows.—Wm. Maris.
2. No. 100. Milking Time.—Wm. Maris.
2. No. 102. Dutch Pasture.—Wm. Maris.
2. No. 103. Duck Pond.—Wm. Maris.
2. Nos. 86 to 89. Four Views of Holland Towns.—K. Klinkenberg.
2. No. 175. Portrait of Queen of Holland.—Hubert Vos.
2. No. 176. Old Women's Almshouse.—Hubert Vos.
2. No. 177. Poor People.—Hubert Vos.
3. No. 178. Angelus.—Hubert Vos.
2. No. 180. Russian Peasant.—Hubert Vos.
2. Nos. 289, 300 and 302. Views in Holland.—J. Weissenbruch.

BELGIUM.

2. No. 49. After the Storm.—Arden.
2. No. 63. Pyramus and Thisbe.—Bourotte.
2. No. 78. Shipwrecked on Holland Coast.—Cogen.
2. No. 90. Herder Assembling His Flock.—De Beul.
2. No. 91. Return to the Stable.—DeBeul.
2. No. 125.—La Porte de Hal in Brussells.—Gailliard.

2. No. 129. One Florin.—Dodding.
1 No. 180. The Dangerous Bridges.—Plumot.
1. No 181. Leaving the Stable.—Plumot.
2. No. 218. Nightfall —Van Damme-Sylva.
1 No. 219. In the Open Air.—Van den Bos.
2 No. 220. Gage of Love.—Van den Bos.
2. No. 230 Return of the Herd.—Van Leemputten.
1. No. 231. End of Autumn —Van Leemputten.
2. No. 239. Le Coup de Collier.—Van Severdonck.

DENMARK.

1. No. 27. Fisherman Returning Home.—Ancher.
1. No. 28. Three Old Fellows.—Ancher.
1. No. 87. Rough Sea at a Rocky Coast.—Blache.
1. No. 49. A Milking Place.—Christiansen.
2. No. 51. Evening Picture.—Dahl.
2. No. 59. Heracles and the Satyr.—Frolich.
1. No. 60. The Satyr.—Frolich.
2. No. 138. Isaac Seeing Arrival of Rebecca.—Pedersen.
2. No. 164. Fishermen.—Taxen.

NEW SOUTH WALES.

2. No. 51. The Prospector.—Ashton.
2. No. 52. After the Shower.—Lister.
2. No. 53. "The Plowman Homeward Plods His Weary Way."—Spence.
2. No. 55. Rounding Up a Straggler.—Mahoney.

JAPAN.

2. Collection of plaster casts, bronzes and marble sculptures.
2. Collection of Japanese water colors (no titles).
2. Collection of paintings on ivory, enamel, porcelain, etc.
2. An eagle carved from wood, and objects carved from ivory and precious stones.

UNITED STATES.

2. **No. 187.** The Angel With the Flaming Sword. —E. H. Blashfield.
3. **No. 188.** Christmas Bells.—E. H. Blashfield.
3. **No. 201.** Passage of the Red Sea.—F. A. Bridgman.
2. **No. 202.** Women at the Mosque.—F A. Bridgman.
2. The Satyr and the Traveler.—Neville Cain.
2. **No. 262.** A Fool's Fool.—Thos. S. Clarke.
2. **No. 264.** A Gondola Girl.—Thos. S. Clarke.
2. **No. 296.** Painting and Poetry.—Kenyon Cox.
2. **No. 305.** Portrait of St. Gaudens.—Kenyon Cox.
2. **No. 306.** Flying Shadows.—Kenyon Cox.
2. **No. 366.** Abandoned.—Chas. H. Davis.
2. **No. 331.** A Winter Evening.—Chas. H. Davis.
2. **No. 333.** The Open Sea.—Walter Dean.
2. **No. 334.** Peace.—Walter Dean.
2. **No. 371.** Monastic Life.—Frank V. Du Mond.
2. **No. 373.** Christ and the Fishermen.—Frank V. Du Mond.
2. **No. 376.** Chrisanthemum Garden.—Fannie E. Duvall.
2. **No. 379.** Mother's Pleasure.—F. Dvorak.
2. **No. 385.** Portrait of Dr. Agnew.—Thos. Eakins.
2. **No. 386.** The Crucifixion.—Thos. Eakins.
2. **No. 389.** Portrait of Dr. Gross.—Thos. Eakins.
2. **No. 429.** Mark Twain (owned by Mr. Clemens). —C. N. Flagg.
2. **No. 468.** A Gregorian Chant.—Walter Gay.
1. **No. 467.** Charity.—Walter Gay.
2. **No. 506.** Light of Incarnation.—Carl Gutherz.
2. **No. 507.** Arcessita ab Angelis.—Carl Gutherz.
2. **No. 522.** In Arcadia.—Alex. Harrison.
2. **No. 523.** The Bathers.—Alex. Harrison.
1. **No. 526.** Twilight.—Alex. Harrison.
2. **No. 527.** The Surprise.—Birge Harrison.
3. **No. 528.** Return of the Mayflower.—Birge Harrison.
2. **No. 534.** On the Way to the Grand Prix.— Childe Hassam.
1. **No. 538.** Indian Summer.—Childe Hassam.

2. No. 560. The Scarecrow.— Geo. Hitchcock.
2. No. 581. Breaking Home Ties.—Thos. Hovenden.
1. No. 582. Bringing Home the Bride.—Thos. Hovenden.
2. No. 584. Return of the Herd.—W. H. Howe.
2. No. 587. Early Start to Market.—W. H. Howe.
1. No. 633. Rent Day.—Alfred Kappes,
2. No. 634. Tattered and Torn.—Alfred Kappes.
2. No. 647. The Strike —Robt. Koehler.
2. No. 653. Behind the Footlights.—Louis Kronberg.
2. No. 650, Asking a Blessing.—A Koopman.
2. No. 671. Great Bridge at Chioggia.—F. W. Loring.
2. No. 687. St. Genevieve.—E. L. Major.
2. No. 690. The Flagellants.—Carl Marr.
2. No. 706. The Witches.—Walter M'Ewen.
2. No. 707. The Absent One.—Walter M'Ewen.
2. No. 713. The Sermon.—Gari Melchers.
2. No. 714. The Pilots.—Gari Melchers.
2. No. 721. Tunis Market.—W. L. Metcalf.
3. No. 761. Pocahontas.—Victor Nehlig.
2. No. 806. The Annunci ition.—Chas. S. Pearce.
2. No. 807. The Shepherdess.—Chas. S. Pearce.
2. No. 811. Love's Token.—Orin Peck.
2. No. 842. Where Waves and Sunshine Meet.— F. K. Rehn.
2. No. 847. Awaiting the Absent.—C. S. Reinhart.
2. No 848.   Washed Ashore.—C. S. Reinhart.
2. No. 911. Sheep Shearing.—Walter Shirlaw.
2. No. 912. Rufina.—Walter Shirlaw.
2. No. 917. The Carpenter's Son.—E. E. Simmons.
2. No. 936. Baptism.—J. L. Stewart.
3. No. 943. Episode of the Revolution.—Julian Story.
2. No. 978. Mother and Child.—F. H. Tompkins.
2. No 1042. In the Lair of the Sea Serpent.— Elihu Vedder.
1. No. 1044. The Fisherman and the Genie.— Elihu Vedder.
2. No. 1052. Mending the Canoe.—Douglas Volk.

2. No. 1055. Bad News.—R. W. Vonnot.
2. No. 1078. Hagar and Ishmael.—Ida Waugh.
2. No. 1079. The Underground Railroad.—C. T. Weber.
2. No. 1081. Two Hindoo Fakirs.—E. L. Weeks.
2. No. 1082. Three Beggars of Cordova.—E. L. Weeks.
2. No. 1083. Persian Horse Dealers.—E. L.Weeks.
1. No. 1095. Portrait of Admiral Farragut.—J. F. Weir.
2. No. 1096. Forging the Shaft.—J. F. Weir.
2. No. 1099. Lady with the Yellow Buskin.—J. M. Whistler.
2. No. 1100. Princess of the Land of Porcelain.— J. M. Whistler.
1. No. 1101. Painting by J. M. Whistler.
1. No. 1102. Painting by J. M. Whistler.
1. No. 1103. Painting by J. M. Whistler.
2. No. 1129. The Celestial Choir.—J. H. Witt.
3. 1152. Grand Canon of the Yellowstone.—Thos. Moran.
2. No. 1153½. On the Road to Santa Fe.—Thos. Moran.
2. No. 1207. Got Him.—Henry E. Farny.
2. No. 1208. Mountain Trail.—Henry E. Farny.
2. 1273. Old Friends.—C. M. McIlhenny.

LOAN COLLECTION.

The loan collection in the United States exhibit consists of pictures by noted foreign artists, owned in the United States. The following are pictures of great merit and value.

3. A Reading from Homer.—Alma Tadema.
3. Reverie.—Bastein Lepage.
3. Sheep. Rosa Bonheur.
3. Colza Gatherers.—Jules Breton.
3. Flight from Sodom.—J. B. Corot.
3. Flight into Egypt.—Cazin.
3. Orpheus.—Corot.
3. The Cooper's Shop.—Daubigny.
3. Flag of Truce.—Detaille.
3. The Pool.—Jules Dupre.
3. Vision of Tannhauser.—Fantin.

3. Beach at Portici.—Fortune.
3. Snake Charmer.—Gerome.
3. A Country Festival.—Knaus.
3. View Near Poissy.—Messonier.
3. Reconaissance —Messonier.
3. Sheep Shearers.—J. F. Millet.
3. The Gleaners.—J. F. Millet.
3· Shepherdess.—J. F. Millet.
3. The Haymaker.—J. F. Millet.
3. Pig Killers.—J. F. Millet.
3. Man with a Hoe.—J. F. Millet.
3. You Are Welcome.—Van Beers.
3. St. Hilarion.—Tassaert.
2. Morning, Noon and Night.— Thos. Shields Clarke.

SCULPTURE.
American.

1. No. 9. The Ghost Dance.—Paul Bartlett.
2. No. 10. Bohemian and Bear.—Paul Bartlett.
1. No. 12. The Secret. (East of the building.)— Theo. Bauer.
2. No. 13. Bas-Relief-Joe Jefferson in His Favorite Impersonations.—Theo. Bauer.
2. No. 16. Tired Out.—J. J. Boyle.
2. No. 26. Buffalo Hunt.—II. K. Bush-Brown.
2. No. 32. The Cider Press.—Thomas Shields Clarke.
2. No. 37. Signal of Peace.—C. E. Dallin.
2. No. 39. Kypros.—John Donoghue.
2. No. 40. Young Sophocles Celebrating a Victory.—John Donoghue.
2. No. 43. Bust of Alcott.—D. C. French.
3. No. 44. Angel of Death and the Sculptor.—D. C. French.
2. No. 45. Bust of Lincoln.—J. Gelert.
2. No. 48. Struggle for work.—J. Gelert.
2 No. 60. Pan.—J. S. Hartley.
2. No. 69. Fighting Panther and Deer. —Edward Kemys.
2. No. 71. The Still Hunt.—Edward Kemys.
2. No. 72. Battle of the Bulls.—Edward Kemys.

2. No. 77.   Christ Crucified.—Henry Kitson.
2. No. 84.   Historical Door of Trinity Church.—
C. H. Nichaus.
2. No. 90.   Shakespeare.—W. O. Partridge.
1. No. —   Alexander Hamilton.—W. O. Partridge.
2. No. 110. Abraham Lincoln.—John Rogers.
2. No. 120. Indian Bear Hunt.—Douglas Tilden.
1. No. 119   Tired Boxer.—Douglas Tilden.
2. No. 124. Love Knows no Caste.—F. E. Friebel.
1. No. 126. The First Fish.—F. E. Freibel.

LOAN EXHIBIT.

3. No. 2989. Cupid and Psyche.—Auguste Rodin.
3. No. 2990. The Sphinx.—Auguste Rodin.
2. No. 2991. Andromeda.—Auguste Rodin.
3. ———   Dickens and Little Nell.—Elwell,

French.

3. No. 11.   Washington and Lafayette.—Bartholdi.
1. No. 15.   Fawn Playing with Panther.—Becquet.
2. No. 25.   Rhinoceros and Tigers.—Cain.
2 No. 26.   Eagle and Vultures —Cain.
2. No 27.   Lion Strangling Crocodile.—Cain.
2. No. 34.   Volunteers of 1776.—Choppin.
2. No. 31.   Joan of Arc.—Chaper.
2. No. 43.   Republican France.—Falguiere.
2. No. 44.   Diana Shooting.—Falguiere.
2. No. 48.   Man of the Stone Age.—Fremiet.
2. No. 49.   The Wounded Dog.—Fremiet.
2. No. 60.   In Danger —Houssin.
2. No. 64.   Immortality.—Hugues.
2. No. 69.   Egyptian Harpist.—Itasse.
3. No. 98.   Herald of Murcia.—Meissonnier.
3. No. 101. Dancing Muse.—Meissonnier.
3. No. 102. Wounded Horse.—Meissonnier.
2. No. 103. David.—Mercie.
2. No. 104. Even So.—Mercie.
2. No. 106. The Blind Man and the Paralytic.—
Michel.
2. No. 107. Fortune Holding Up Her Diadem.—
Michel.

2. No. 110. An Idyl.—Mombur.
2. No. 118. The Return.—August Paris.
2. No. 132. Burgess of Calais.—Rodin.
2. No. 135. Hero and Leander.—Rongelet.
2. No. 136. Spirit Guarding the Secret of the Tomb.—Saint-Marceaux.
2. No. 137. A Conqueror.—Sanson.
3. No 146 to 184. Casts of French sculpture from 11th to 19th century.
3. No. 255. Voltaire.—Houdon.
3. No. 254. Diana.—Houdon.
3. No. 256 and 257. Animals.—Barge.

German.

3. No. 4. William I.—Baerwaldt.
2. No. 6. Bust of Moltke.—Begas.
2. No. 15. Eve.—Brutt.
2. No. 16. Saved.—Brutt.
2. No. 24. Thornpuller.—Eberlin. •
3. No. 33 Moses Destroying the Tables of Law; carved from oak.—Herter.
2. No. 35. Christ and the Daughter of Jairus.—Helgers.
3. No. 36. Model of the Dusseldorf Warriors' Monument.—Hilgers.
2. No. 40. Echo.—Hultzch.
2. No. 53. Death's Embrace.—Klein.
2. No. 66. Emperors William I and Frederic III; in zinc —Manthe.
2. No. 72 and 73. Emperors William II and III.—Oches.
2. No. 95. Victory.—Siemering.
3. No. 96 to 98. Statues of Bismark, Moltke and Crown Prince Frederic, loaned by National gallery of Berlin —Siemering.
2. No. 105. Resting Herdsman.—Toberentz.
3. In the exhibit of architecture is a model of the new Parliament building at Berlin.

Italian.

1. No. 5. Bathing Woman.—Albacini.

1. No. 10. Bust of Julia Ward Howe —Apolloni.
2. No. 15. American Mythology.—Apolloni
2. No. 29. Fraternal Love.—Calzalari.
2. No. 32 Surprise.—Canonica.
2. No 56. Christopher Columbus.—Galli.
2 No. 61. The Fisher Boy.—Lavezzari.
2 No. 76. Faun and Bacchanti.—Soeboeck.
2. No. — Sappho.—Adelaide Mariani.
2. No. 81. Last of the Spartans.—Trentanove.
2. No. 83 Indian Warrior.—Tronbeskoy.
2. No. 23. The Arts (6 statuettes).—Bottinelli.
2. No. 88. Lincoln Dying.—Ferrari.
2. No. 89. Rebecca.—Zocci.
2. No. 73. The Poor Flower Girl.—Ramazotti.

Swedish.

3. No. 4 Linneas —Eriksson.
2 No 5. "1779."—Eriksson.
2. No. 7. The Snowdrop.—Hasselberg.
2. No. 8. The Frog.—Hasselberg.
3. No. 16. The Lion of Gothia.—Nystrom.

Brit sh.

2. No. 4. The Pearl.—Miss Brown.
2. No. 10. Henry Irving as Hamlet.—Ford.
2. No 11. Gladstone.—Ford.
2. No. 13. Caprice.—Frampton.
2. No. 14. Singing Girl.—Frampton.
2. No. 25. Needless Alarm.—Sir F. Leighton.
2. No. 26. The Sluggard.—Sir F. Leighton
1 No 30. Boy Catching Crab.—Miss Montalba.
2. No. 32. Birth of Venus —Montford.
2. No 38. Egyptian Harpist.—Rhodes.
2. No. 39. Youth's First Recognition of Love —
Rhodes
2. No. 43. The Mower.—Thorycroft.
2. No. 44. Fencer.—Thorycroft.
2 No 46. Putting the Stone.—Thorycroft.
2 No. 49 to 52. Busts of Tennyson, Carlyle, Cardinal Newman and Gladstone.

NOTE.—The exhibits from Spain, Mexico, Nor
way, Costa Rica, Brazil, Algeria, and several other
countries were not open May 23, when this book
was put in press.

LA RABIDA MONASTERY.

The Rabida Convent is a fac-simile of the original monastery near Palos, Spain, which was erected in the second century. It is situated east of the Agricultural building, south of the Casino and just north of the Krupp gun. It contains 1,067 relics of Columbus and other things pertaining to the discovery of America, the exhibit surpassing, in historical interest, anything on the fair ground. The exhibits are described by their numbers, it being impossible to locate them intelligibly, owing to the peculiar arrangement of the building. The following features are of paramount interest and deserve high grade.

No.   —

1. Model of Norse ship supposed to have been used by Leif Erikson in his voyage to America.
6. Chart showing location of houses built by Leif near Boston
10. Fac-simile of inscriptions on Dighton Rock, said to have been carved by Norsemen in 10th century.
11. Fac-simile of Icelandic Sagas of 14th century.
12A. Portrait of Kublai Khan, who is said to have visited America in the 13th century.
13. Picture of statue of Leif Erikson, who is claimed to have discovered America in 10th century.
14. Published volumes relating to discovery of America by the Norsemen.
19. Copy of a letter from Toscanelli made by Columbus on fly leaf of a book.
20. Portrait of Marco Polo.
24. Portrait of Claudius Ptolemy, the first great geographer.
24. Copy of 1475 edition of Ptolemy's Cosmographia, used by Columbus.
28. Fac simile of pages of " Historia Reram

Ubique Gestarum," with marginal notes in handwriting of Columbus.

29. Fac-simile of pages of "De Imago Murdi," with marginal notes in hand writing of Columbus.
35. Arms and armor of time of Columbus.
45. Curious maps of 15th century.
56. Portrait Queen Isabella.
59. Portrait of King Ferdinand.
61. Original of will of Isabella, made Nov. 23, 1594.
63. Crown of Isabella.
65. Missal, treasure chest, scepter and sword of Isabella.
104. Statue of Isabella at Malaga.
110A. View of the harbor and city of Genoa.
112. House at Quinto where father and mother of Columbus lived.
113. Street in Genoa where Columbus was born.
116. Room in which Columbus was born.
128. Church at Porto Santo, where Columbus used to reside.
131. Block of Carbosana wood from house occupied by Columbus
131. Interior of room occupied by Columbus and his wife at Funchal.
133. Table made of wood from house at Funchal occupied by Columbus.
134. Cane made from wood from house of Columbus at Porto Santo.
136. Relics from house of Columbus at Porto Santo.
141. View of the monastery of La Rabida.
142. Columbus at monastery gate.
144. Columbus at La Rabida.
146. Columbus asking bread at La Rabida.
151. Columbus explaining his theories at the monastery of La Rabida.
153. Columbus explaining his theories to the Prior.
155. Cloisters of convent at La Rabida.
157. Room occupied by Columbus in monastery of La Rabida.
165. Columbus before the Dominicans at Salamanca.
172. Columbus before the Junta.
174. Present appearance of house at Salamanca in

325. Fragments of horse shoes used in time of Columbus.
326. Santiago, Santo Domingo, where first gold was found by Columbus.
344. Wood from tree of Columbus, Santo Cerro.
345. Old bell from Santo Cerro.
363. Native canoes from Santo Dimingo.
365. Fragments of ancient horse-shoes used on horses of Columbus' men.
373. Autograph letter of Francisco Roldan, 1502, that caused Colum' us to be brought home from Santiago in chains.
375. Columbus imprisoned by Bobadillo.
376. Columbus returning to Spain in chains.
383. Photographs of chains placed upon Columbus by Bobadilla.
389. Pieces of wood from beam to which Columbus was chained.
384. Enlarged fac-similes of inscriptions on chains worn by Columbus.
390 Letter of Columbus to nurse of Don Juan.
392. Piece of timber from house of Columbus at Santo Domingo.
398. Reception of Columbus by Isabella on return from third voyage.
417. Street in Truxillo near place where Columbus first landed on American continent.
420. Present appearance of place where Columbus first landed in Honduras.
444. Columbus receiving presents from wife of the Cacique.
447. Burial of an Indian princess.
456. Strange animals seen by Columbus.
471. Bell of Carthagena.
493. Autograph of Columbus, 1502.
492. Page of "De las Proficias," a book written by Columbus.
495. Death of Columbus.
497. House in which Columbus died.
498. Chapel of convent of Cartrya, in which Columbus was buried.
507. Tomb of Columbus and steps to the Presbytery.

508. Fac-simile of box in which remains of Columbus were found.
510A. Fac-simile of casket in which dust of Columbus rests.
510B. Fac-simile of the " Urna" enclosing casket of Columbus.
511. Replica of doors to cell in which are held remains of Columbus.
513. Autograph of Bartholomew Columbus written in 1508.
517. Autograph of Don Diego, son of Columbus.
526. Genealogy of Columbus family to the present day.
551, Autographs of Columbus.
552. Signature of Columbus.
553. Autograph letter of Columbus to the Catholic Kings.
563. Photograph of votive offerings left at shrine of Virgin at Siena by Columbus.
566. Coins made of first gold brought from America.
570. Bolt to which Columbus was chained in dungeon at Santo Domingo.
600. Fac-simile of title page of first book published about America.
609. Letter of Columbus to Luis Sant Angel.
621. The first published portrait of Columbus.
631. First book in English concerning America.
640. Log book of Columbus.
670. Portrait of Americus Vespucci.
697. Matthias Ringman, who carried from Paris to Saint Die the letter of Americus Vespucci, which, when translated, christened the New World.
727. Map, A. D. 1500, representing North America as a collection of islands.
763. Ancient Dutch map showing Greenland and eastern shore of New World.
801. Montezuma, emperor of Mexico.
802. Portrait of Cortez.
803. Fac-simile of sword of Cortez.
808. Great idol of the Aztecs.
814. Portrait of Pizarro.

816. Atahualpa, last of the Incas.
819. Early pictures of America from De Bry's voyages, 1595.
827. Fac-simile of two signatures of Pizarro.
828. Standard of Pizarro.
844. The fleet of Magellan.
845. Portrait of John Cabot.
846. Sebastian Cabot, discoverer of North America.
849. Sir Walter Raleigh.
853. Sir Francis Drake.
867. St. Augustine, Florida, in 1565.
901. Original commission given to Columbus by Ferdinand and Isabella upon his departure for first voyage.
935. Will of Columbus.
937. Letter from Columbus to the Pope.
957. Letter of Columbus to Ferdinand and Isabella.
967. Original " Capitulation" of Columbus with the Spanish sovereigns.
968. Original autographic statement by Columbus of gold brought by him from America and sold in Castile.
970. Original draft by Columbus for one hundred gold castellanos.
971. Original draft by Columbns.
972. Fragment of envelope with seal of Columbus and writing in his own hand.
974. Signature of Columbus as Viceroy.
990. Letter from the Pope, Sept. 20, 1448.
991. Bull of the Pope, May 3, 1493.
993. Bust of Pope Alexander VI.
1000. The Ribero chart, made in 1529.
1001. Large map on vellum, made in 16th century.
1002. The Borgian map of America, made in 1529.
1003. Picture, "St. Peter Weeping," from museum of the Vatican.
1005. Picture, " The Roman Forum."

LEATHER BUILDING.

Dimensions, 150x575 feet.   Cost $100,000

Exhibits mentioned are located by sections and numbers.

1. Oxide leather—M 1.
1. Glazed kid—M 8.
1. Sole leather—M 9.
1. Leather machines—N 9.
1. Fargo's exhibit of shoes—N 23.
1. Hanan & Sons exhibit of shoes—N 25
1. Ladies' fine slippers—N 27 to 31.
1. Alligator skins—O 1.
1. Swift & Co.'s exhibit—P 3.
1. Lambean leather—P 7.
1. Boston Rubber Shoe Co. exhibit—P 9.
1. Walker Oakley's exhibit—P 15.
1. Patent leather—Q 2.
1. Parisian leathers and shoes—O 19 to 25.
1. Blacking and dressing—L, M, N, O, P, Q and R 34.
1. Lynn, Mass., shoe exhibit—L, M, N, O, P, Q and R 35.
3. Collection of shoes from foreign countries on west side of building.
2. Machines in operation on second floor turning out 1,000 pairs shoes per day.

FORESTRY BUILDING.

Dimensions, 208x528 feet. Cost, $100,000.

Iron has not been used in the construction of this building; wooden pins take the place of bolts and rods. It is surrounded by a row of tree trunks with the bark on, each state in the Union being represented in the row by three trees. ' The exhibits listed below will be found without difficulty. A large aisle runs from north to south. On the east side of this aisle are sections A and B; on the west side, sections, C and D. Entering at the north, begin with section B and go south on east side; then return on west side.

SECTION B.

3. Oregon spruce.
1. Pennsylvania woods.
1. Wisconsin red cedar.
1. Minnesota woods.
1. Kentucky exhibit.
1. Ohio medicinal plants and polished woods.
1. Michigan. Model of sugar camp in Michigan forty years ago. Miniature log cabin in case.

SECTION A.

1. West Virginia exhibit.
1. Missouri exhibit. Woods finished and unfinished.
1. California polished woods.
2. Woods of the United States, from the Jessup collection in the American Museum of Natural History, New York.
2. Cabin made of cork.
2. Redwood plank from Humboldt county, California, 16 feet, 5 inches wide; 12 feet, 9 inches long, and 5 inches thick.
2. The E. D. Albro collection of polished woods. Section of mahogany from Tobasco, Texas.

SECTION C.

1. Manufactured articles of wood.
1. Connecticut exhibit.
1. French veneered woods and collection of cones.
2. Trunk of first tree planted under timber culture patent No. 1, 1877.

SECTION D.

2. New South Wales polished woods.
1. Mexican exhibit.
1. Brazil exhibit.
1. German exhibit. Large and small casks.
1. Paraguay exhibit.
1. Wigwam of bamboo.

HORTICULTURAL BUILDING.

Dimensions, 250x998 feet. Cost, $300,000.
In order to specify location of exhibits, the building will be divided as follows: Dome; North Curtain of Dome; South Curtain of Dome; Dome Gallery; North Section West Side; South Section West Side; North End; South End.

DOME.

1. Miniature mountain and pyramid of shrubbery under dome.
3. Crystal cavern under mountain.
3. Traveler's tree (*Ravenella Madagascariensis*).
2. Century plant.
1. Euphorbia Elegans.
1. Pandanus Veitchii, or screw pine.
2. Aurucaria, or Australian pine of unusual size.
2. Rhododendrum of unusual size from Versailles, France.

2. Sago palm showing unusual quantity of leaves.
2. Cactus collection, with specimens of "Old Man's Head."
2. Large specimens of Areca Sapida.
2. Model of Capitol at Washington in Cape of Good Hope flowers.
3. Crown top bay laurels, exhibit of M. F. Gallagher.
2. Climbing palm (*Plectocomia Assamica*).
2. Gallagher's collection of plants and shrubs.

SOUTH CURTAIN.

3. Remarkable collection of orchids, among them the Cattleya Mossiar, Cypropedium Odontoglossum and Orcidum.
2. Collection bromelias.
2. Anthurium, or tail flowers.
1. Hydragias; colors changed by searing root with hot iron.
1. Cape jasmines.
3. Collection Dracæna Massangeana (of dragon's blood tree family).
2. Large Farleyence Adiantum.
2. Tree ferns; among them the Platycorum, or elk horn.
1. Three varieties of asparagus—Plumosum, Tennissimus and Pitcherianus.
1. Begonias Rex.
1. Specimens Crotons.

NORTH CURTAIN.

1. Asphidestra from Toronto.
3. Egyptian paper plant (*Papyrus Antiquorum*), from which the papyrus of antiquity was made.
2. Japanese miniature garden. Collection of maples and arbor vitae.
2. Japanese fern roots of natural growth in peculiar shapes.
2. Japanese collection peonies.
1. Cereus cacti bed from Central America.

DOME GALLERY.

1. Photo. views of Botanical gardens, New South Wales.
1. Japanese garden ware.
1. New York collection fungi.
2. Crystal fountain and cave.

NORTH SECTION—West Side.

1. Canadian fruits.
1. New Mexico fruits—large bunches of grapes.
1. Missouri fruits and vegetables.
1. Idaho pears and apples.
2. Oregon pears weighing 3 lbs. 10 oz. each. Apples without blemish. Prunes.
1. Colorado fruits.
2. Washington fruits and vegetables. Apples and pears. Churchill potato 15 inches long, weight 5 lbs. Strawberry 11 inches in circumference. Yellow egg plums. Hungarian prunes.
1. Florida oranges and Peento peaches.
2. Cocoanut tree, bearing.
1. Pineapple plant.

NORTH END.

1. New South Wales dried and preserved fruits and jellies.
1. Canned goods, garden seeds, tools, implements and machinery.

SOUTH SECTION—West Side.

1. Australian pears, apples and grapes.
1. Oranges and lemons from Palermo, Italy.
2. Tower of oranges and lemons from Los Angelos county, Cal.; 14 feet at base, 36 feet high.
1. Placer county, Cal., cherries and Lorquot plums.
1. San Diego county, Cal., fruits,
1. German artificial fruits.

1. Illinois fruits.
1. Minnesota peaches.
1. Michigan artificial fruits and vegetables.
1. New Jersey fruits.
2. New York—165 varieties apples.
1. Wisconsin fruits.
2. Liberty Bell made of oranges from Los Angelos county, Cal.

SOUTH END.

3. Bark tree containing California wine exhibits.
1. Huge bottle from Rheims.
1. Wines of France, Spain, New South Wales, California and other states.

WOMAN'S BUILDING.

Dimensions, 199x388 feet.   Cost, $138,000.

2. Portable weaving machine and other inventions of women.
1. Exhibit of Blue Anchor society of New York, showing relief work done by women for wrecked sailors.
1. The several parlor exhibits showing decorative treatment.
2. Mrs. Candace Wheeler's decoration of the library.
2. Exhibit of the Cincinnati Pottery Club.
2. Marble fountain made by Anne Whitney. Bust of Lucy Stone by same artist.
3. Statue of dragon which surmounted the State House in which the Continental Congress held sessions in 1877.

2. Wax figures showing style of dress since **A. D.**, 1400.
2. Feather opera cloak made by woman of South Dakota.
1. Buffalo skins tanned by squaws.
2. Collective exhibit of Associated Artists, New York. Decorative work.
1. Embroidered table linen made by women for Marshall Field & Co.
3. Gold and steel embroidered work done in Denmark in 1794.
2. Shawl made by woman 100 years old.
2. New York exhibit of laces and embroidery.
1. Embossed leather work; chairs, etc.
3. Three pieces of marble statuary by Vinnie Ream Hoxie.
3. Statuette by Edmonia Lewis, the colored sculptress
2. Painted tapestries made by women.
3. Crayon of Napoleon I, from life.
2. Exhibit of training schools for women, New York and Philadelphia.
2. North American Indian exhibit.
3. The Keppel collection of engravings, etchings, etc., by celebrated artists from 1535 to 1835.
2. Curious and useful things from the Cape of Good Hope.
3. Several paintings by Queen Victoria and other women of the royal house.
3. Specimens of handiwork by Queen Victoria.
2.· Exhibits of poker work, repousse wood carving, etc., done by women.
2. Chairs, stools etc. sent by Royal School of Art Needlework, London.
2. Library of books written by women.
3. Irish industries, in charge of the Countess of Aberdeen.
2. Women's industries from New South Wales.
2. Decorative work by Countess Di Braza, Italy.
2. Japanese exhibit. Articles made by ladies of the court.
2. Exhibit made by Russian women, including

work by the Grand Duchess and other ladies of rank.
2. Unique exhibit from Siam.
2. Tapestries, laces and art and literary exhibit by the women of Sweden.
2. Model kitchen.
2. Bas-Relief in marble, by Sara Bernhardt.
2. Statue of Psyche, by Mme. Bertaux.
3. Statue of Lief Erickson, by Anne Whitney.
2. Statue of Miriam, by Vinnie Ream Hoxie.
2. Exhibit of book covers and illustration from New York Bureau of Applied Design.

FISHERIES BUILDING.

Dimensions, 165x365 feet, with two polygonal annexes, each 134 feet in diameter, connected by arcades. Cost, $224,000.

Begin at west end of main building and go east on south side of main aisle; then come back on north side of main aisle.

MAIN BUILDING.

1. Model of Irish fisheries school.
1. Australian exhibit of shells and aquatic specimens in alcohol.
1. Canadian exhibit of preserved fish.
2. Gloucester, Mass., exhibit; types of fishing vessels and implements in use since 1623.
1. Cast of sword fish weighing 390 lbs., captured in Boston Bay in 1872.
1. San Diego, California, stuffed birds, fishes, etc.
1. Minnesota inland fishes.
1. Holland preserved fish. Fishing scene in miniature.

1. Japanese preserved fish and prepared edible aquatic plants.
1. North Carolina fish and aquatic birds.
1. Rush camp used in mullet whale fishing.
2. Washington state exhibit. Skeleton of hump-back whale, 47½ feet long, maximum girth 40 feet.
1. Russian exhibit of fishing implements and preserved fish.
2. Norway exhibit. Huge polar bear. Model hatching station. Model of fishing station. Fish oils and preserved fish.

EAST ANNEX.

3. Large fountain in center with rare and beautiful fishes swimming in basin.
3. Rows of glass tanks, capacity 140,000 gallons, containing great variety of fresh and salt water fish.

WEST ANNEX.

1. Angling paraphernalia—rods, reels, hooks, boats, etc.
1. Exhibits of Pennsylvania and Wisconsin State Fish Commissions.
1. Folding boats.

MAN OF WAR "ILLINOIS."

Length over all, 358 feet. Length of water line, 348 feet. Breadth, 69 feet. Mean draught, 24 feet. Cost, $100,000.

3. Owing to shallow water no man of war could be harbored at the World's Fair; consequently the model stationary ship Illinois was constructed of brick, iron and wood. It is almost an exact model of the man of

war Oregon. Located on lake shore, opposite Government building.

GUN DECK.

1. Six-inch naval guns.
1. Rapid firing machine guns.
1. Projectiles.

SPAR DECK.

1. Conning tower, wheel, rudder indicators, speed indicators. Batteries of rapid firing machine guns.

MAIN DECK.

1. Models of U. S. war ships.
1. Ship dispensary and hospital.

NAVAL MUSEUM.

1. Projectiles of all sorts.
2. Old gun picked up by man of war near Newport, Rhode Island.
1. Small guns built at Annapolis by cadets. Naval scenes. Portraits of the U. S. navy admirals.
1. Naval Hydrographic department.
1. Surveying instruments.
1. Officers' quarters.
1. Naval Academy. Books used in instruction of students.
1. Fish torpedoes.
1. Projectile torpedoes.
1. Ammunition hoists, showing interior of ship's turrets.
1. Berth deck with ship's stores.

U. S. Naval Lake Front Exhibit.

Located on lake front, near man of war "Illinois."

1. Tested armor plates.
1. Light house 100 feet high, with winding stairs leading to tower.

NAVAL OBSERVATORY.

2. Chronograph, registering standard time to fraction of second.
1. Chronometers of all kinds

LIFE SAVING STATION.

1. Life boats and cars.
2. Rocket line apparatus and rocket firing.
2. Metallic life car which has saved 201 lives.
1. New style life car.
1. Life line box.
1. Cork jackets. Pins for coiling the life line.

DAIRY BARNS.

Located between White Horse Inn and Cliff Dwellers.

2. Barn No. 1.—43 Jersey cows., 'Lilly Flag" valued at $15.000, from Huntsville, Ala., record, 1.047 lbs., of milk in one year. "Eurotisimo," owned by D. F. Appleton, Ipswich, Mass., record, 958 lbs. of milk in one year. "Lillie Goldie" owned by C. I. Hood, Lowell, Mass..record, 34 lbs., 4 ounces in one week. "Betty Marchioness," owned by Walter W.

Law, New York city. "Phebo Rex." owned by Theodore A. Havermeyer, New York city. "Hugo Countess," owned by D. L. Heinsheimer, Glenwood, Io. " Merry Maiden," owned by C. & O. Graves, Mailland, Mo., "Little Alteration," owned by W. E. Matthews, Huntsville, Ala. "Annice Wagnet," owned by John Boyd, Chicago. "Signal Queen," owned by Frank Eno, Pine Plains, N. Y. "Brown Bessie," owned by H. C. Taylor, Oxfordville, Wis. "Lorita" owned by J.J.Richardson, Davenport, Io. "Pearl of Riverside" owned by H. A. Huntington, Nashville, Tenn.

2. Barn No. 2.—34 Guernsey cows. "Maturna" valued at $15,000, owned by N. K. Fairbank, Chicago, record, 10,000 lbs., of milk in ten months. "Select 8th," from noted strain, heavy milker. "Countess Cora" and "Countess Bella of the Tonilets," imported cows. "Rosette 5th," "Lady of Ellerslie," "Essence" "Rosabella" and "Mina 3d" from ex Vice-President Morton's stock-farm on the Hudson. "Lawntennis," heavy milker. "Claudia." "Miss Cowslip."

2. Barn No. 3.—30 Short-horn cows. Imported Bashford of Storm Lake, Io. "Genevive of Kansas." "Waterloo Daisy," of York, Ontario. "Nora," of Osage, Io. "Royal Duchess," of Glauntsworth, Canada.

Dairy Building.

Located near Cliff Dwellers.

1. Latest devices for making butter. Cold storage appliances for milk and cream. Cheese factory, showing new process. Electric motors for running dairies.

LIVE STOCK PAVILION.

Dimensions, 280x440 feet. Cost, $335,000. Located south of agricultural building.

Kennel exhibit begins June 12 and continues six days.

Exhibit of cattle and horses begins August 21 and continues thirty days.

Exhibit of sheep and swine begins Sept. 25 and continues twenty days.

Exhibit of fat stock and poultry begins October 16 and continues twelve days.

Anthropological Building.

Dimensions, 225x415 feet. Located in southeast corner of the grounds, near Forestry building.

This building, as its title implies, is devoted to Man and His Works. At this time the exhibits have not been placed, but within a few weeks it will be one of the most interesting features of the Fair. Within the building will be found relics of primitive man from all parts of the world; skeletons of prehistoric men; implements and ornaments used by the human family thousands of years ago; skeletons of animals extinct for ages; idols; ruins of temples, and hundreds of other articles of great historical interest. On the outside will be located several Indian villages, the inhabitants illustrating the life led by them in their primitive state.

United States Indian School.

This building is near the Krupp gun structure.

1. Architectural plans of houses made by Indian pupils.
2. Thirty-one Indian pupils—20 boys and 11 girls —from Albuquerque, New Mexico, representing five tribes.
2. School in session. Carpenter shop. Harness shop. Shoe shop. Girl's working room.
1. Cases of things manufactured by Indians.

ADMINISTRATION BUILDING.

The administration building covers a space 262 feet square, in the form of four pavilions each 84 feet square. The grand central dome is 277 feet high and 120 feet in diamater at the base. Cost of building, $550,000; is coated with aluminum bronze, the material for which cost more than $50.000.

Pavilion A contains the offices of the United States commissioners, telegraph office, and messenger service.

Pavilion B is occupied largely by the executive officers of the Fair; also, custom house officers.

Pavilion C, bureau of information and publicity, offices of local newspapers and correspondents.

Pavilion D. In this section are located the office of foreign affairs, the bank, express company and guards.

Cold Storage Building.

2. This building is located south of the Sixty-fourth street entrance. It is intended to show the manner of ice manufacture and the method of producing cold air by the ammonia process. Refrigerating machines will be shown in operation. The upper portion of the building will be devoted to a skating rink, of ice newly made every day. This building will furnish the ice for all uses on the fair grounds during the Exposition.

Choral Building.

2. The organ used in the choral building is a four manual instrument with an echo organ at the rear of the auditory, controlled from the organist's seat. The organ is valued at $25,000.

Statuary.

There are about one hundred and fifty sculptural groups and figures of heroic size in the park.

2. Benjamin Franklin; 16 feet high; cost, $3,000. Stands in the main entrance of the electricity building.

2. Republic; 60 feet high; on pedestal 40 feet high; cost $25,000. Stands at entrance to the basin from Lake Michigan.

3. Grand Fountain; 150 feet in diameter; cost $50,000. Stands at the head of the basin. Its waters can be illuminated by electricity.

Music Hall.

North end of Peristyle.

1. 130x250 feet; finest accoustic properties for orchestral purposes of any hall in America; seats 2,500.

The Wooded Island.

The wooded island contains sixteen acres and is devoted to floriculture, horticulture and the Japanese exhibit. The Imperial Japanese commission is located on the north end of the island. Near this building is a group of Japanese cottages, decorated in the highest style of native art. On the extreme south end of the island is located the hunter's cabin of the Boone and Crocket Club, and a miner's cabin from New South Wales.

Japanese Tea House.

2. The Japanese tea house and garden, north of the Fisheries building, illustrate the ancient art of polite tea drinking. In the garden choice tea is served to the public by Japanese in the native style. ''Tea ceremonies'' are conducted by Japanese women in a Japanese summer house. Antique ware is shown in the summer house.

2. Two porcelain garden lanterns, several pieces of antique bronze, and a number of other relics are shown in the garden.

2. Tea plant 150 years old in garden.

Michigan Logging Camp.

2. Southeast of Agricultural building. Dimensions, 24x70 feet. Made of hemlock and Norway pine. Complete reproduction of Mich. logging camp.

Old Kentucky Distillery.

2. Reproduction of an old Kentucky distillery in full blast. A continuously running still, capacity 500 gallons a day; bonded ware-house and government offices.

Puck Building.

Location, north of Horticultural building.

2. Entire process of editing and printing World's Fair *Puck.*

FIRST FLOOR.

1. Six Hoe presses, each printing a different color; transfer press; stone grinder.

GALLERY.

1. Artists' and engravers rooms; type setting; making lithographic stones.

Cliff Dwellers.

Location, southwest of Krupp Gun Building, Exterior represents a mountain and canon with trees and grasses growing on their sides; also ruins of cliffs. Fire-proof throughout. Interior represents canons with Cliff Dwellers' houses on sides and blue sky overhead.

3. West end—Ruins of Cliff Dweller's palace (an exact reproduction of ruins found in Colorado, scale 1-10.)

3. Balcony house (exact.)

3. South Side—Square tower (exact). Mountain trail up to well and balcony.

3. Interior—Exact reproduction, full size of "Estufa," or Cliff Dwellers' living-room with cooking utensils and other implements as found by explorers.

3. Burro trail up the mountains. Live pack mules or burros saddled and climbing ruins, guarded by a ram remarkably intelligent and able to cope with any wild beast.

2. Cave opening from south central side lighted with electricity and containing rare paintings of Cliff Dwellers' ruins from studies made in the west (exact).

2. Museum with the only complete collection of Cliff Dwellers relics in the world, opening from North central side, containing the following notable things, among many others: Sandals of willow, knives and drills of stone, bows and arrows, spoons and awls, axes of stone, poniards, "baby boards," corn grinders of stone, mats, leather moccasins.

3. Corn over 1,500 years old, in bulk and on cobs, found in a room over which a tree had grown 1,000 years old—age of tree shown by number of its rings. Scientists have experimented with samples of the corn and made it grow by the aid of electricity.

3. Squash seeds and rinds, bean seeds same age as
    corn.
2. Bowl of walnuts just as found, 1,200 years old.
2. Turkey-feather cloth. Leggins. Implements for
    lighting fire. Loom needles. Material woven
    with hemp and human hair. Fine woven cot-
    ton cloth.
3. Forty skulls of extreme antiquity. Stone door
    slab. Six foot skeleton of man with large skull.
    Skeleton of female with withered flesh on
    bones. Mummy in feather cloth. Six foot
    skeleton with flesh on. Mummies of child
    and infant. Hand 2,000 years old with flesh
    on. Mummy in matting, showing mode of
    embalming. Exhibits of hair exactly as found.
2. Stone lamps. Crockery. Pottery. Ladles and
    spoons. Rings. Pot with hunting scene on it.
    Huge fire pots and wooden shovels.

Specialties.

Whaling barque Progress. Located at the south
pond.

A museum illustrating the whaling industry; also marine curiosities and relics. Admission 25 cents.

Electric Intramural Railway. Elevated railway
about Jackson Park. 20 cents for round trip

Movable side-walk, long Pier, Jackson Park.
Electrically propelled side walk. Five cents a ride
from the shore to the end of the side-walk.

Venetian gondolas and barques, about lagoons
and basins, with gondoliers. Round trip 50 cents.

Electric launches. Transportation through lagoons and basins. Round trip 50 cents.

Steam Launches. Transportation through outer lagoons, basins and Lake Michigan. Round trip 25 cents.

Wheel chairs. Roller chairs about grounds and buildings. 75 cents an hour with attendant; 40 cents an hour without attendant.

An enclosure at the extreme northwest corner of the grounds contains the Esquimaux village. Besides men, women and children from the Esquimaux country, there are a number of dogs, used for sledding. There is a small lake within the enclosure, where the natives give exhibitions in their canoes. Fishing and hunting implements are shown. An admission fee of 25 cents is charged to this exhibit.

The Children's building is located between the Horticultural and Woman's buildings. Here children will be fed and cared for by trained nurses while their mothers visit other parts of the ground.

FOREIGN BUILDINGS.

A number of foreign buildings have not yet been completed. In the following list will be found all that are open at this time.

Krupp Gun Building.

Location, near lake shore, east of Agricultural Building

3. In center of building, "Krupp's Baby" one of the largest guns in the world, for coast defense; 48 feet long, 17 inch bore, weighs 140 English tons; carriage weighs 150 English tons; shoots 20 miles and has pierced steel plates 2 feet thick at 9 miles; each projectile costs $12,000, weighs 2,500 lbs. and is 5 feet long.

2. Four Man of war guns—70 ton, 12 inch bore; 50 ton, 9 inch bore; 25 ton, 8 inch bore; 15 ton, 7 inch bore.

1. Three guns—6 inch bore, 4 inch bore and 3 inch bore.

1. Five screws for man of war. Two hundred projectiles of all kinds. Big wheel 40 feet in diameter and shaft 80 feet long. Five steel plates shot through at five miles.

German Building.

Located on lake front, north of man of war "Illinois." Cost $400,000. Architecture of the early Renaissance period.

---

2. Chime of three bells on southwest part of roof, from Bazbum on the Rhine; rung on state occasions and holidays during the fair.

INTERIOR.

2. Chapel containing following groups of statuary: Meyer's life-size group in wood illustrating the the crucifixion scene. Schulter's groups in terra cotta showing Christ on the cross.

1. Panels illustrating birth and crucifixion of Christ.

MAIN HALL.

1. Meyer's Statuary in cream and white, blue and gold.

1. Schulter's statue of St. John.
2. Extensive library of rare German works, embracing some of which no duplicates can be found.
1. Corner with antique German furniture.
1. Paintings by celebrated German artists.
1. Mammoth clock.
1. Old manuscripts.
1. Rare musical works.

East Indian Building.

Located in northwest corner of grounds.

2. Indian temple or shrine.
2. Figures of Buddha.
1. Figures representing religious mendicants.
1. Platters of brass with designs representing scenes in the life of Krishna.
1 Figure of Krishna, seated on back of beast representing entwined bodies of milkmaids.
1. Figure of Ganesha.
1. Stories of Hindoo mythology illustrated in wood and stone and on brass and silk.
2. Copies of famous monuments of India.
1. Table tops, trays, boxes and placques, inlaid with precious stones.
2. Incrusted metal ware.
2. Tusks of ivory carved in lace patterns.

French Colonies Building.

Located near Cliff Dwellers.

2. This is a picturesque building, with all of its

interior ornaments carved by hand. The windows a·e of stained glass in curious patterns.
1. Indo China silks.
1. Guadeloupe and Martinique mats, fabrics and curios.
1. Tunis native woods, barks, mats and native garments.
2. Tunis and Algerian building with natives selling their wares. Idols from Indo China. Silver and lacquered ware. Curiosities from the Congo, the Antilles and French Indies. Products of mines. Wines. Fabrics of all kinds.
1. Moorish cafe.

Swedish Building.

1. Built of brick and timber from Sweden. Interior—View of Capital. Exhibits of Swedish sports, ships, etc. Winter scene. Old Swedish rooms with occupants in costume. Modern Swedish home. Statue of Gustavus Adolphus. China and pottery. Woman's work. Gold, silver, tin and glass ware. Iron. School exhibit on second floor.

Turkish Building.

Located north of the Fisheries building.

1. Special exhibits of the products of the Orient, among which are a case of rugs and a case of valuable embroidered and painted silks.

Costa Rica Building.

1. Woods, birds, and curios.

STATE BUILDINGS.

Several of the state buildings are incomplete at this date (May 24), and others contain nothing of special interest. The buildings that have not yet been opened will probably have exhibits worth seeing. The following list includes all buildings now open to the public.

Massachusetts.

Cost, $75,000. Modeled after the old colonial homestead of John Hancock.

2. In main hall: Copies of charters granted by King Charles and William and Mary.
1. East room, done in old Dutch kitchen style. Portraits of Gov. Winthrop, William Pynchon, 1657, Benjamin Franklin, Catharine M. Smith, 1697.
1. Northwest room. Portraits of John Adams, John Quincy Adams and famous generals.
1. Southwest room. Portraits of early governors. Picture of Roger Williams' house.

SECOND FLOOR.

1. Main hall: "Last Indian of Nantucket" and other pictures.
2. Book of autograph sermons, 1755. "History of the fight at Concord, 1775." Sperm candles, 1776. Map made in 1651. Card table, 1790. Embroidery made in 1740 by Mary Parsons, aged 10 years. Old state papers. Rare old portraits of Gen. Putnam, Washington and Warren.

3. Remnant of Mrs. Gov. Bradford's wedding dress, 1623. Picture brought from Canterbury by Puritans. Gov. Hinkley's chair, 1634. Chair from oldest Congregational church in Plymouth, 1730.
1. West room : Bust of Jared Sparks. Autograph letters of noted authors, poets and statesmen. Portraits of Mann and Channing.
3. Desk of George Washington. Puritan writing desk brought to Plymouth by John Drew in 1660. Old colonial chairs and tables.
1. West bed-chamber: Fac-simile of original Harvard college charter. Commission of Col. Wm. Prescott.
2. Case of dresses over 150 years old worn by celebrated persons on notable occasions.
2. Case of revolutionary and colonial relics. Doll 100 years old. Slippers 1750. Shingle with bullet hole made in Revolutionary war. Spectacles, 1730. Iron smoking pipe, 1693. Spoon, 1745. Candle that came from England in the *Speedwell.* Bonnets of 1800. Christening cap worn by Dr. Byles as a baby in 1706.
3. Case of relics: Quilt made from pieces of Lady Washington's dresses. Silk from Mrs. John Hancock's ball dress. Court suit worn in 1776 by Dudley Cotton. Silk skirt of Mrs. Hancock. Embroidered waistcoat of Gov. Hancock.
2. Philadelphia *Packet* of July 8, 1776, containing notice of reading of Declaration of Independence. Pencil sketch of Washington in 1790, from life. Ancient painting by Copley. Pictures engraved by Paul Revere. "Landing of British troops" and "Bloody Boston massacre."
2. Case of relics: Autograph letter of Washington. Old portraits. Old French map of Boston. Contract of John Pickering for building first church in Salem. Salem antiquities. Epitaph of Benjamin Franklin in his own hand, 1706. Autograph letters of Gen. Warren, William Bradford and William Pence
2. Old band-boxes.

3. Cradle in which five generations of the Adams family were rocked.
2. Fire-screen with painting of John Hancock's colonial home, given by Hancock to Samuel Adams. Mirror used by Gov. Hutchinson.

Illinois.

Dimensions, 160x470 feet.   Cost, $250,000.

In listing exhibits the order taken in each aisle was from center of building towards outside doors.
1. West wing, main floor, first aisle to the north: Grotto and rustic bridge. Native woods. Agricultural palace. Farm scene made of grasses and grain.
1. Center aisle, north side: Forestry display. Agricultural exhibit.
1. Center aisle, south side: Pressed brick. Minerals. Agricultural implements of stone age. Floral display.
2. First aisle to south of center aisle: Stratigraphic series.
2. Relics of Mound Builders. Pipes and idols.
1. Last aisle to south: Various kinds of soil. *Mollusca.* Indian arrow-heads. Pottery of Mound Builders.
1. East wing, north aisle: National history exhibit. Electrical machinery. Wood work.
1. Center aisle, north side: Architectural exhibit. High school exhibit. Elgin Columbian school made in paper blocks by children.
1. Center aisle, south side: State university exhibit. Grain exhibit. Stock farm exhibit. Photographs. Drawings. Writings. Zoölogy.
1. First aisle to south: Native silk industry. Needlework. Clinton county flag.
1. Last aisle to south: Palette club art exhibit.

Chicago Art Institute exhibit.
1. Southeast corner of building: Kindergarten room.
1. Northeast corner of building: High school methods illustrated.
1. To left of south entrance: Reception room of Illinois Woman's board. Art exhibit.
1. Gallery, east wing: State Institution for Deaf and Dumb exhibit.
1. Stairway, south of dome: Art display of Illinois Woman's board.
3. Bell presented to Catholic church at Kaskaskia by King Lewis of France, 200 years ago. It was the first bell heard west of the Alleghenies.

Pennsylvania.

Dimensions, 100x166 feet.   Cost $300,000.

.GROUND FLOOR.

3. In hall: Old Liberty Bell.
1. In southeast room: Oil paintings.
1. In east hall: Full length portrait of Washington in worsted.
1. In grand reception room: Large painting, group showing Gen. Washington, Col. Tighlman, Gen. St. Clair, Col. Alexander Hamilton, Gen. Anthony Wayne, Baron DeKalb and other Revolutionary heroes.
1. In northeast room: Stained glass window.
2. In southwest room: Paintings done by Pennsylvanians in Paris.
1. At head of main stairway: Large painting, "Birth of our Nation's Flag."

SECOND FLOOR.

1. In southwest (Governor's) room: Paintings, " Sunrise on Pike's Peak;" "Sunset on Medieval Castle."

2. In hallway (west side): Rare portrait of William Penn by Richardson 1684–1699.

2. Philadelphia room at head of stairs: Case of curiosities—Lutheran hymn book, 1772. Ale mug of John Paul Jones. Vest, stockings and watch worn by Chas. Carroll when he signed Declaration of Independence. John Hancock's sword. Flint lock taken from gun on English frigate. Anthony Wayne's sword.

2. Jefferson's sword, and chair in which he sat while writing Declaration of Independence. Ink and pen used in writing same.

2. Washington's sofa and wash bowl. Old Masonic certificate of membership to Geo. A. Barker, 1796.

1. Pictures of William Penn and wife, Washington, mayors of Philadelphia and others. Historical document of Pennsylvania society for abolition of slavery.

1. In correspondents' room: Painting of Old John Burns of Gettysburg. Map of Pennsylvania in relief.

1. Exterior of building: Tower, an exact reproduction of that on Independence Hall.

1. Pennsylvania coat of arms over main entrance. Statue of Penn and Franklin, front facade.

Connecticut.

Dimensions, 73 x 73 feet. Cost, $12,000. Reproduction of colonial residence.

FIRST FLOOR.

3. Gun with which Gen. Israel Putnam shot wolf in cave.

1. Portrait of Putnam. Flint-lock guns used in Revolutionary war. Painting of Charter Oak.

SECOND FLOOR.

2. In Windsor room: Chair of "Parson Newell,"

1730. Bedstead of mahogany, 250 years old. Spread worked in 1743 by Rachel Hill-house. Bed curtains 175 years old. Chintz covered chair, 1740. Oak chests, 200 years old.

2. In south chamber: Reproduction of Wethersfield room where Washington slept. Case of colonial relics. Curtains brought from England in 1706.

1. In New Wethersfield chamber. Dressing case, 1793. Chair of Gov. Sessions, 1746.

2. In Charter Oak chamber: Oak leaves and acorns stenciled on walls. Chair 150 years old. Old clock.

1. In main hall: Collection of relics.

New Hampshire.

Dimensions, 53 x 84 feet. Cost, $25,000. Reproduction of Swedish castle.

2. Case of relics: Spade used by British in throwing up intrenchments at Saratoga. Silver-mounted pistols worn by John Langdon at Saratoga. Brass candlestick used by Gen. Stark at battle of Bennington. Bullets used in first outbreak of Revolution in New Hampshire.

2. Spectacles of 1722. "Pilgrim plate," 1797. Sleeve buttons of 1778. Flint-lock used during Revolution. Baby's cap 100 years old. Silver porringer of Gov. Plummer, 1748.

2. Counterpane 150 years old. Ivory painting, 1780. Satin christening blanket, 1780. Spoon, 1743. Child's plate, 1630. Wedding ring. 150 years old. New Hampshire *Gazette* of Jan. 27th, 1764. Communion cup, 1660.

2. China set, 1640. Bible used in 1698. Powder horn carried at Bunker Hill. Mrs. John Adams' wedding slippers.

2. Daniel Webster's decanter and autograph letters. Continental money.

Washington.

Dimensions, 118 x 208 feet.   Cost, $100,000.

1.   In front: Flag staff of red fir 208 feet high.
1.   In south wing: Red fir block 9 feet in diameter.
     Largest cedar vase ever turned from one piece
     of wood.
1.   Wood exhibit.
1.   In main hall: Reproduction of farm.   Wheat
     pyramid 19 feet high, 101 bushels to acre.
2.   Largest mammoth skeleton ever found.
1.   In north wing.   Art and school exhibits.
2.   Block of coal weighing 26 tons.

California.

Dimensions, 144 x 435 feet.   Cost, $300,000.

2.   Century plant in bloom in front yard, south.
2.   Main floor: Mineral exhibit. $10,000 in prec-
     ious metals.   Native gold quartz.   Diamonds.
     Translucent onyx.   First nugget of gold found
     in state.
1.   North wing: Orange bearing trees.   Colossal
     horse made of dried fruits.   Statue, "Cali-
     fornia."
1.   In gallery: Historical exhibit.

New York.

Dimensions, 105 x 160 feet.   Cost, $77,000.

2.   John Boyd Thacher's wampum exhibit—Por-

tion of Hiawatha wampum, commemorating the federation of the Five Nations. Part of the Long House wampum, commemorating treaty of 1784. Fragment of wampum commemorating time when Indians first saw whites.

1. Ladies' parlor in green and gold, on first floor. Parlor in white and gold with fine frescoes, on second floor.

Virginia.

Cost, $25,000.

1. An exact representation, inside and out, of the home of Washington at Mt Vernon at the time of his death. Rooms are as follows: First floor—State banquet hall: music room of Miss Custis (Washington's niece); Washington's dining room. Second floor—Room in which Washington died, with furniture in room at the time; Lafayette's room; Nellie Custer's chamber; Green room. Pictures and furniture are the originals from Mt. Vernon.

New Jersey.

Cost, $20.000. Exterior and interior are exact reproduction of Washington's headquarters at Morristown.

1. Main room: Reproduction of Washington's writing table in mahogany. Mahogany distaff. Book case. Clock. Old fashioned fire place.

1. Second floor: Copy of Washington's wine buffet with cut glassware. Washington's bedchamber with chintz covered furniture. Washington's dining room.

Iowa.

Dimensions, 77 x 123 feet.   Cost, $50,000.

FIRST FLOOR.
2. Ceiling and wall decorations in corn.
1. Miniature coal palace.
1. Collection Iowa soils.
1. Miniature flax palace.
1. Miniature Iowa capital in grain.

SECOND FLOOR.
1. Dutch bible printed in 1686.
1. Portrait of Black Hawk.

Ohio.

Dimensions, 80x100 feet.   Cost, $100,000.

1. On front lawn: Group of Ohio statesmen in bronze.
1. On first floor: Portraits of President Hayes and Gen. Sherman. Art exhibit in Cleveland ladies' parlor. Toledo and Hamilton parlors.
1. Banquet hall on second floor.

Maryland.

Cost, $20,000.

1. First floor: Piece of the mulberry tree under which Leonard Calvert made treaty with

Indians in 1633. Representation of Chesa-
peake Bay in tank. Oyster house and oyster
craft. Paintings.
1. Furniture 100 years old on second floor.

Minnesota.

Dimensions, 78x91 feet. Cost, $50,000.

1. Main floor: Art exhibit. " Indian Massacre."
Minnehaha Falls.
1. Fauna and flora.
1. Second floor: Collection of Indian relics. Rare
old French painting.

Indiana.

Dimensions, 100x150. Cost, $75,000.

1. Miss Nettie Scudder's statue, "Indiana."
1. Sisters of Mary art collection. Paintings of the
state's governors and public men.

Florida.

Dimensions, 137x137 feet. Cost, $100,000. A
reproduction of Fort Marion, built by Hugenots at
St. Augustine in 1620.

1. Sea shells. " The Pinto Peach." Palms and
grasses.

Delaware.

Dimensions, 58x60 feet.   Cost, $10,000.

1.   Art display.   Thomas F. Bayard's collection. Work of native artists.   Picture of oldest church in America.

Maine.

Dimensions, 65x65 feet.   Cost, $40,000.   Built of 9 varieties of Maine granite.

1.   Paintings, " Bar Harbor.''   " Casco Bay.'' Long-fellow from life in 1840.   "Georgie Cayvan.''

West Virginia.

Dimensions, 34x76 feet.   Cost, $20,000.

3.   Sofa on which Grant and Lee sat at Appomattox while discussing terms of Lee's surrender.

Wisconsin.

Dimensions, 80x90 feet.   Cost, $65,000.

1.   Six thousand dollar stained glass window at head of stairs.
1.   History of state framed, 8x12 feet.

Michigan.

Dimensions, 100x140 feet. Cost, $100,000.

1. Stuffed wolverines. Art exhibit. Map of state in Saginaw room.

Kansas.

Dimensions, 125 x 138 feet   Cost, $100,000.

1. Scene in the foot hills. Grain exhibit. Deer, bear, etc.

Idaho.

Cost, $20,000. .Built of Idaho cedar and native lava stone.

1. Third floor: Exhibit of minerals, animals and sage brush. Roof garden.

Nebraska.

Dimensions, 60 x 100 feet. Cost, $50,000.

1. Grain exhibit. Woman's work. Art. Wood carving.

Colorado.

Dimensions, 45 x 125 feet.   Cost, $12,000.

1.   Art exhibit.

Missouri.

Dimensions, 86 x 86 feet.   Cost, $150,000.

1.   "Star chamber."   Walls done in minerals.
Frescoes.   Statue of Spring.

Montana.

Dimensions, 62 x 113 feet.   Cost, $50,000.

1.   Art exhibit: "Shoshone Falls at Sunset."
Indian Scenes."

Utah.

Dimensions, 46 x 82 feet.   Cost, $10,000.

2.   Archaeological exhibit.   Mummies of cliff
dwellers.

North Dakota.

Dimensions, 50 x 60 feet.   Cost, $25,000.

1.   Grain exhibit.

Vermont.

Reproduction of Pompeiian villa.   Cost, $15,000.

1.   Statuary.

MIDWAY PLAISANCE.

A narrow strip of land nearly a mile in length. extending west from the north end of Jackson Park, is known as the Midway Plaisance. It is a part of the Chicago park system, and joins Jackson and Washington parks. Here are located the amuse- ment features and other specialties of the fair which do not properly come within the scope of the main exposition.

2. Java village. Sarongs, Kreises, silver work.
2. Samoa village. Big war canoe. mats, cloth. etc.
1. Dahomeyan village.
1. Captive balloon.—Balloon ascensions: elevation 1 500 feet. two trips an hour. Admission to enclosure 25 cents: trip in balloon $2 Each p ssenger making ascension is entitled to photograph of party.
1 Barre Sliding Railway—10 cents a ride.
1. Dutch East India Village.—Palkees and other native vehicles for transportation. Prices to be approved by Committee on Ways and Means
3. Ver'ical Revolving Wheel.—The wheel is 250 feet in diameter and 237 feet in height: 50 cents for ride of two round trips.
1. Constantinople Street scene.—Turkish Theater (two performances daily), admission 50 cents: Persian tent. admission 25 cents; panorama. Syrian photos, admission 25 cents: Turkish restaurant, native musical performances tribe of Bedouins, admission 25 cents.
1. Cairo Street.—Egyptian amusements, native dancing, snake charmers, fortune-tellers, con- jurors, musical and theatrical performances, collections, photos, pictures and paintings, wedding processions and mouled; admission until 11 a. m. 25 cents, reserved seats 25 cents;

after that hour free. Egyptian temple, admission 25 cents.

1. Dutch East India Village—Two theaters (one in each side of street), exhibitions by native bands, jugglers, snake charmers, dancers (male and female), and other characteristic entertainments. Admission fees to be approved by Committee on Ways and Means. At present, admission 25 cents.

2. German Village and Town of Medieval Times.— German and Bavarian bands in connection with restaurant, museum of curios, antiquities, and works of art peculiar to Germany. Admission, 25 cents. German tribes representing house of the Upper Bavarian Mountains, Black Forest or Alsatian, the Allman Tribe, the Hessian or Altenburg House of Silesian Bauren, Middle Germans, Westphalian Hof of the Lower Saxons, etc. Such tribes and houses to constitute the village.

1. Natatorium.—Natatorium with musical performances. Admission, with use of baths, 50 cents.

1. Moorish Palace.—Exhibit and sale of native goods, chamber of horrors, trip through Switzerland, trip to the moon, camera obscura representatives in wax, etc. Moorish Palace, right to exhibit $1,000,000 in gold coin. Café in connection. Admission to amusement features, 25 cents.

1. Panorama of Bernese Alps.—Scenery of Switzerland ; admission, 50 cents.

1. Panorama of Volcano of Mount Kilauea.— Painting to faithfully reproduce in miniature the volcano action of the crater of Mount Kilauea ; admission 50 cents.

1. Algerian Village.—Algerian village. Tunis, and Algeria streets and bazaars, etc., concert hall, café, Kabyle House, tents, etc ; admission 25 cents.

1. Hungarian Concert Pavilion and Café.—Musical entertainments, theatrical performances,

gypsy bands, native performers in native diess; admission, 25 cents.

1 Venetian Glassware and Mosaics.—Factory in full operation, sale of Venetian and Florentine wares. Admission, 25 cents.

2. Chinese Village.—Chinese village, theater with native performers. Joss house and Chinese tea garden and café. To theater and Joss house admission 25 cents.

1. Irish Village and Blarney Castle.—Representing ruins of Blarney Castle, exhibit and sale of Irish products by natives.

1. Persian Building.—Exhibit and manufacture and sale of distinctively Persian gcods. Musical entertainments, etc., native artisans and performers; admission 50 cents.

1. Costumed Natives of Forty Countries.—Exhibit of natives, appropriately costumed, from at least forty of the countries of. the world; and photographs of same; admission 25 cents.

1. Typical Irish Village with Native Inhabitants. —Admission 25 cents.

1. Japanese Bazaars.—Manufacture and sale of Japanese articles; native attendants. No admission fee.

1. Vienna Café and Concert Hall.—Restaurant with musical performances. No admission fee.

1. Model of St. Peter's Church, Rome.—Admission 25 cents.

2. Hagenbeck's Zoölogolical Arena.—Exhibition of wild animals, etc. Admission to building 25 cents. Seats in amphitheater from 25 cents to $1.

1. Model Eiffel Tower.—Model to be twenty feet in height. Admission 25 cents.

1. Electric Scenic Theater.—Showing a landscape or other scenes under the changing light as a day passes. The effect being produced by a multitude of various colored electric lights. Admission 25 cents.

1. East Indian wares.—Exhibition and sale of native wares. No admission fee.

MAPS.

On the following pages will be found maps of the Exposition grounds, Midway Plaisance, and city of Chicago.

KEY TO MIDWAY PLAISANCE.

33. Adams Express Co.
16. Algeria and Tunis.
4. American or Indian Village.
7. Austrian Village.
30. Bohemian Glass Co.
6 Captive Balloon.
8a. Chinese Village & Theater.
8b. Chinese Tea House.
32. Circular R R. Tower.
5. Dahomey Village.
1. Depot.
24. Dutch Settlement.
34. Exhibit of Irish Industries.
15. Ferris Wheel.
17. Fire and Guard Station.
13. French Cider Press.
21. German Village
26 Hagenbeck Animal show.
12 Ice Railway.
3. Indian Village.
25. Japanese Bazaar.
29. Libby Glass Co
35. Model of St. Peters.
19. Moorish Palace.
9. Morocco Exhibits.
23 Natatorium.
14 Nat'l Hungarian Orpheum.
2. Nursery Exhibit.
22 Panorama of Bernese Alps.
10. Panorama of Volcano. Kilanean.
31. Persian Concession.
27. R R Station.
11. Roman House.
18. Street in Cairo.
20. Turkish Village.
28. Venice Murano Co.

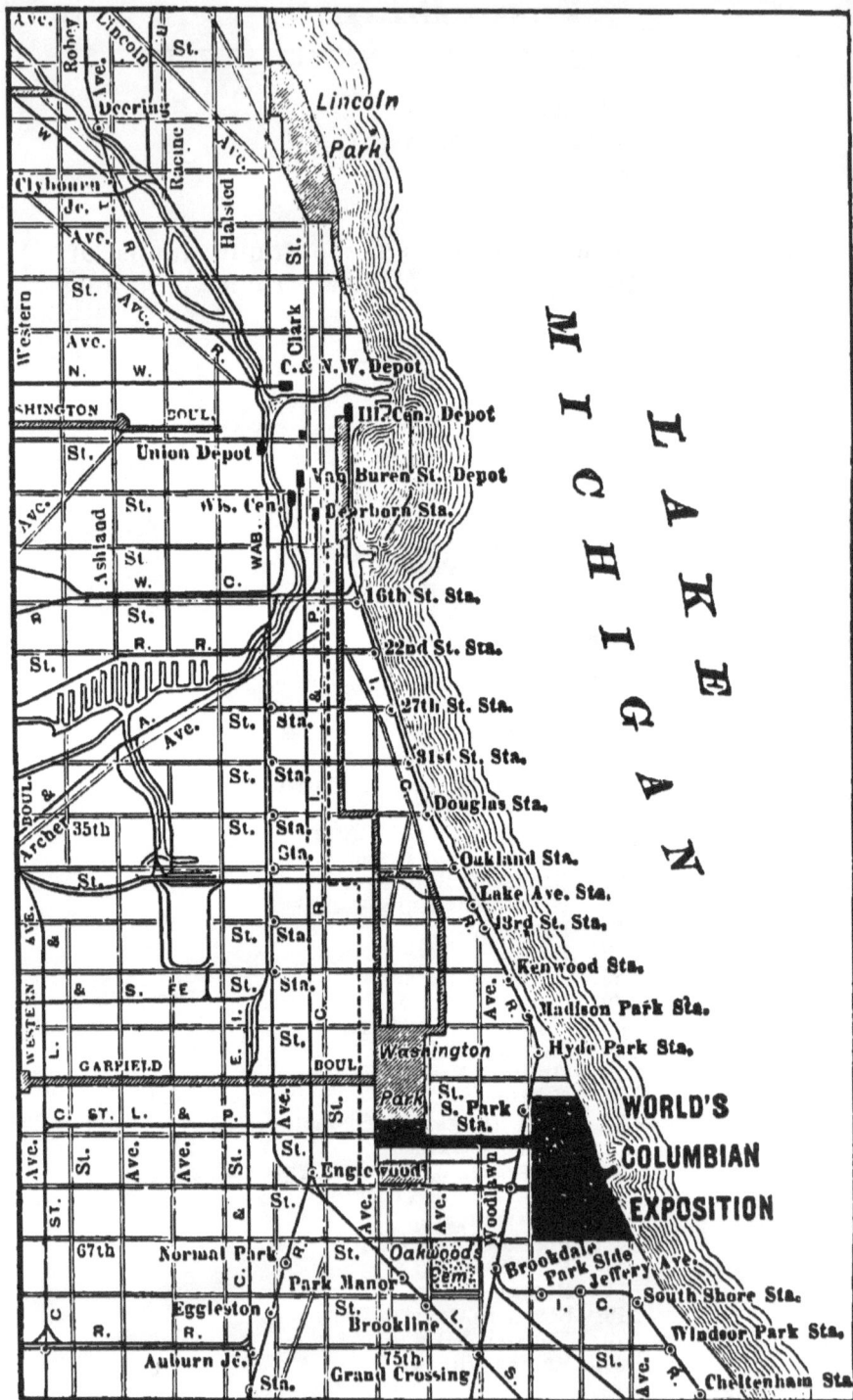

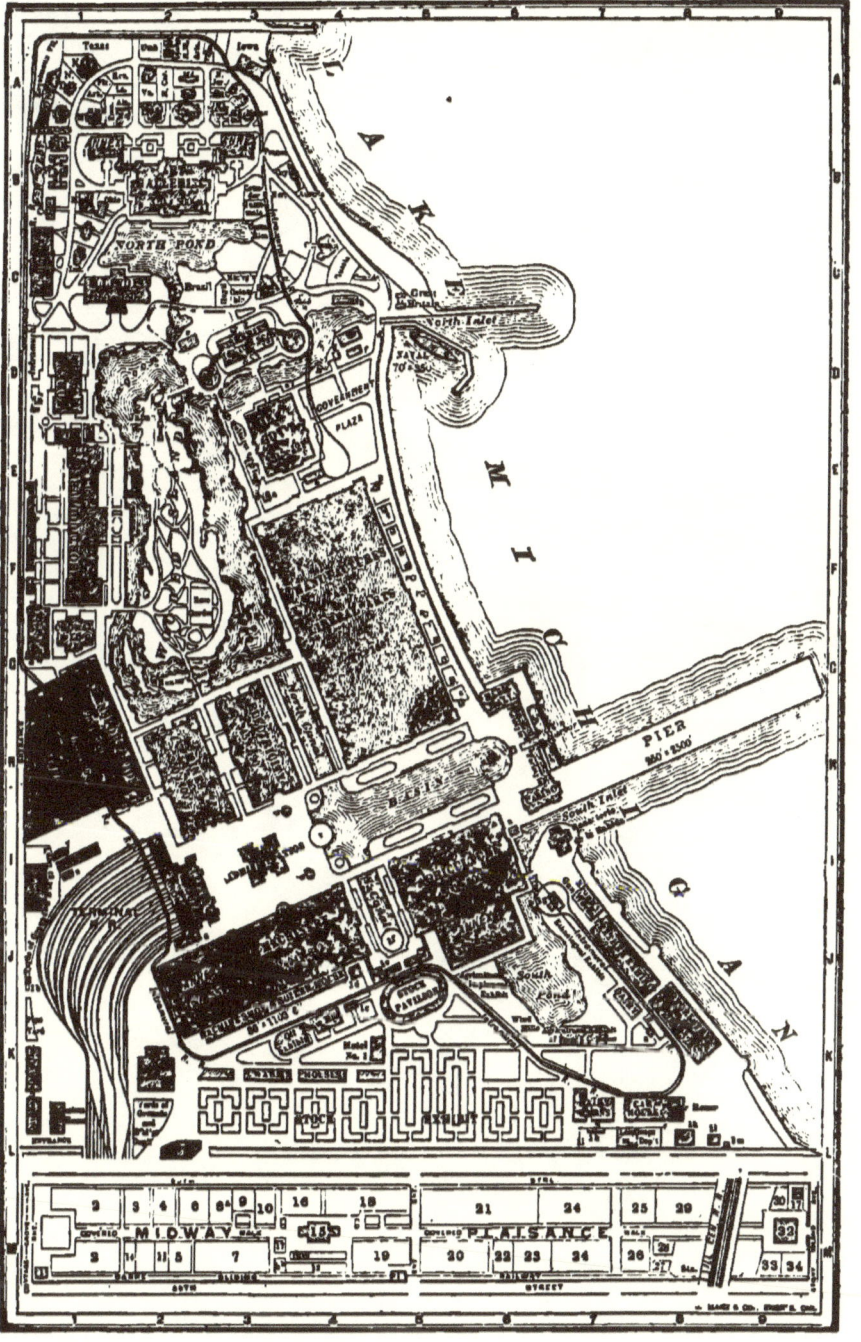

INDEX.

www.ingramcontent.com/pod-product-compliance
Lightning Source LLC
Chambersburg PA
CBHW032148010726
47493CB00008BA/2624